Mariah couldn't stop the memories.

She'd park behind the barn, and he'd run out to meet her. She'd barely be out of her car before he'd pull her into his arms and kiss her.

She glanced at Shane. The look in his eyes told her he was remembering, too. Suddenly he drew her close again. "You were every teenage boy's fantasy."

Hearing his confession, her pulse raced. Mariah hadn't the strength to pull away. She hated her weakness for this man.

D1538391

Dear Reader,

Working with talented writers is one of the most rewarding aspects of my job. And I'm especially pleased with this month's lineup because these four authors capture the essence of Silhouette Romance. In their skillful hands, you'll literally feel as if you're riding a roller coaster as you experience all the trials and tribulations of true love.

Start off your adventure with Judy Christenberry's *The Texan's Reluctant Bride* (#1778). Part of the author's new LONE STAR BRIDES miniseries, a career woman discovers what she's been missing when Mr. Wrong starts looking an awful lot like Mr. Right. Patricia Thayer continues her LOVE AT THE GOODTIME CAFÉ with *Familiar Adversaries* (#1779). In this reunion romance, the hero and heroine come from feuding families, but they're about to find out there really is just a thin line separating hate from love! Stop by the BLOSSOM COUNTY FAIR this month for Teresa Carpenter's *Flirting with Fireworks* (#1780). Just don't get burned by the sparks that fly when a fortune-teller's love transforms a single dad. Finally, Shirley Jump rounds out the month with *The Marine's Kiss* (#1781). When a marine wounded in Afghanistan returns home, he winds up helping a schoolteacher restore order to her classroom…but finds her wreaking havoc to his heart!

And be sure to watch for more great romances next month when Judy Christenberry and Susan Meier continue their miniseries.

Happy reading,

Ann Leslie Tuttle
Associate Senior Editor

Please address questions and book requests to:
Silhouette Reader Service
U.S.: 3010 Walden Ave., P.O. Box 1325, Buffalo, NY 14269
Canadian: P.O. Box 609, Fort Erie, Ont. L2A 5X3

PATRICIA THAYER

Familiar Adversaries

SILHOUETTE *Romance*®

Published by Silhouette Books

America's Publisher of Contemporary Romance

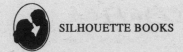 SILHOUETTE BOOKS

ISBN 0-373-19779-9

FAMILIAR ADVERSARIES

Copyright © 2005 by Patricia Wright

Books by Patricia Thayer

Silhouette Romance

Just Maggie #895
Race to the Altar #1009
The Cowboy's Courtship #1064
Wildcat Wedding #1086
Reilly's Bride #1146
*The Cowboy's Convenient
Bride* #1261
*Her Surprise Family #1394
**The Man, the Ring, the
Wedding* #1412
†Chance's Joy #1518
†A Child for Cade #1524
†Travis Comes Home #1530
The Princess Has Amnesia! #1606
†Jared's Texas Homecoming #1680
†Wyatt's Ready-Made Family #1707
†Dylan's Last Dare #1711
**A Taste of Paradise #1770
**Familiar Adversaries #1779

Silhouette Special Edition

Nothing Short of a Miracle #1116
Baby, Our Baby! #1225
*The Secret Millionaire #1252
Whose Baby Is This? #1335

Silhouette Books

Logan's Legacy
What a Man Needs

*With These Rings
†The Texas Brotherhood
**Love at the Goodtime Café

PATRICIA THAYER

has been writing for sixteen years and has published over twenty books with Silhouette. Her books have been nominated for the National Readers' Choice Award, Virginia Romance Writers of America's Holt Medallion, Orange Rose Contest and a prestigious RITA® Award. In 1997, *Nothing Short of a Miracle* won the *Romantic Times* Reviewers' Choice Award for Best Special Edition.

Thanks to the understanding men in her life—her husband of thirty-plus years, Steve, and her three grown sons and two grandsons—Pat has been able to fulfill her dream of writing romance. Another dream is to own a cabin in Colorado, where she can spend her days writing and her evenings with her favorite hero, Steve. She loves to hear from readers. You can write to her at P.O. Box 6251, Anaheim, CA 92816-0251, or check her Web site at www.patriciathayer.com for upcoming books.

My cousin and best friend Connie,

You were there when I caught my first frog,
and got my first boyfriend...and the second and the
third.... The wonderful memories are endless. Although
many miles separate us, you're always in my thoughts.

And always, Steve.

Chapter One

If this wasn't the worst day of his life it was damn close.

Early Monday morning Shane Hunter turned off the highway onto the dirt-and-gravel road. Immediately the old truck's lack of suspension had him bouncing in the seat. He eased his foot off the gas and steered to avoid the potholes. He released a breath as he glanced at the billboard sign that read Paradise Estates in bold letters. In the corner was, in smaller type, By Hunter Construction. He couldn't help but feel pride. Barely two years ago he'd started the company, and now he was building the first phase of Haven, Arizona's, newest housing development. Thirty-five single-family homes. Every dime he had or could borrow was wrapped up in this project. And if luck and the weather held Hunter Construction was on its way.

His life would be nearly perfect if only he didn't have to work for Kurt Easton. There wasn't a resident of Haven who hadn't heard about the Easton family's ongoing feud with the Hunters.

From the very start, Easton had done everything he could to push Shane off the project, especially after there had been two break-ins at the site. Not much damage was done the first time, but in the second incident several pieces of valuable equipment had been stolen. Shane hired more security, but Easton wasn't satisfied. He'd persuaded investors to hire a project manager to keep the project on schedule and to keep an eye on Shane.

Shane drove past the first row of the framed two-story structures. Farther down were several stacks of lumber and building supplies behind a chain link fence. He continued on to the construction trailer where he spotted his crew standing around outside. Shane checked his watch. It was after 7:00 a.m. What was going on? His crew knew their jobs. He'd given the supervisor the list of assignments last Friday. He parked his truck, climbed out and went straight to the framing foreman, Rod Hendon.

"Rod, why is everyone standing around?"

The foreman shook his head. "It's not my call, Shane. The project manager said to wait until you got here."

Shane's stomach knotted, and he had to fight to keep his cool. Easton would love to see him blow up over this. "Where is this project manager?"

Rod pointed at the trailer. "Inside. And I'll tell you right now, you aren't going to like what you find."

Shane didn't doubt it, but over the weekend his brother, Nate, had convinced him that he'd need to keep a cool head if he wanted to complete this job. Shane marched off toward the trailer. Fine, he'd work with a manager, but first they needed to get a few things straight and the sooner the better.

Shane climbed the wooden steps, pulled open the door and stepped inside. "What the hell gives you the right to keep my crew from starting work?" He froze when he found a woman, not a man, sitting behind his desk.

She was an auburn-haired beauty with pale, creamy skin, and a wide, inviting mouth with full, kissable lips. And when she looked up at him with those large green eyes he could only find enough air in his lungs to breathe out her name. "Mariah…"

"Hello, Shane," she said in that soft husky voice he could never get out of his head for the past dozen years. "It's been a long time."

Not long enough to forget. He watched as she came around the desk. At five-eight, Mariah Easton was absolute perfection. She filled out a pair of faded jeans nicely. Too nicely. She wore an oversize chambray shirt that showed off her delicate frame but also hid the generous curve of her breasts. But he knew they were full and lush. *Whoa. Don't go heading down memory lane. You'll only get into trouble.* He shook his head and returned to the present.

"If you're waiting for your father, he isn't here."

Mariah shook her head, causing her wild mane to move against her shoulders. "I've already talked with Dad this morning. He would have been here but I told him I wanted to handle this on my own."

He didn't like the sound of this. "Handle what?"

"I'm the new project manager."

This *was* the worst day of his life. "The hell you say."

Shane knew that Easton could play dirty, but no way would he ever let his precious daughter within ten feet of a Hunter, especially the no-good Hunter boy he'd run off years ago.

Even though Mariah had had a week to prepare for this meeting, she was still nervous. Working in the construction business she'd become accustomed to men staring at her, making off-color remarks, but this man could make her blush with just a look. How had she let her dad talk her into this? The last thing she needed was Shane Hunter back in her life. How many rejections could a woman take anyway?

She tried not to look at him, but Shane had always been hard to resist. He was six foot three and built solid. The years of heavy work had only toned his muscles. But to her it was his deep-blue eyes and that wicked grin that could melt her on the spot. Somehow she had to find a way not to think about how sexy he was and focus on business.

"If you'd like to see my credentials and job experience…" She picked up the folder off the desk and handed it to him. "I just finished a large project in Phoenix. You can call Dad. He'll tell you that his partners approved me for the position." She drew a breath, trying to slow her rapid pulse. "Looks like we'll be sharing this office."

"Now I know your father is crazy." He didn't open the file. "We've already had enough setbacks, and having you oversee my crew isn't going to help. How do you think the men are going to react with you trying to take over?"

Mariah's anger flared, but she held it in check. She had worked very hard to earn a good reputation in this business. "I'm not trying to take over. I'm here to make things run a bit more smoothly. And I've found in the past that the men don't like a woman on the site because of their boss. As the boss, you need to lead the way. If you make it clear that we have a good working relationship, your men will follow your example in dealing with me."

He still didn't look convinced. "You're also one of the investors' daughter."

"Look, Shane, I know you and my father have never gotten along, but for the sake of this project, we need to come to an agreement."

"What a concept. A Hunter and an Easton working together."

She knew her father had held a grudge against his family for years. Was it too much to ask that they put their personal feelings aside? "Shane, if I hadn't accepted this job, they'd just find someone else. It won't take long for word to get around that Hunter Construction is difficult to work with, especially with the problems you've had recently."

His eyes flashed. "We're no different from any project this size. Things get stolen and kids break in and vandalize a site. There hasn't been much damage."

Mariah sat down on the edge of the desk. "You can't be too cautious, even radical environmental activists have been known to vandalize and destroy property. This site does cut into a scenic view."

Shane tossed the folder on the desk. "And that's what will sell these high-priced homes—the view. People will be lining up to purchase them. But not if we let the crew stand around."

"Then let's get them back to work." She raised a hand. "Introduce me to your crew and confirm my job description."

He folded his arms over his massive chest. "And just what will your job be?"

"Most of my duties will be handled from here. I'll order materials, make sure there's no waste and see that supplies are delivered when promised. My job is to bring the project in on time and on budget."

"I thought that was my job."

"It is," she confirmed. "I'm just here to help you. This is a big project, and there should have been a manager from the beginning."

"I like to work alone."

That hadn't changed over the years. Shane Hunter hadn't needed anyone, especially her. It hadn't helped matters that her father hadn't wanted her anywhere near a Hunter. Even now she knew Kurt Easton hoped that Shane and Hunter Construction would screw up this large and very important project.

"Then you have a problem, Shane, because I'm here...to stay." She went to the door. "Now, shall we go outside so you can introduce me to the crew."

He stood there a long time. She decided he needed a little nudge. "Okay, it's your money we're wasting while they stand around," she said. "And it's your butt on the line with the investors."

"Damn, if you're not one stubborn woman." He started for the door; she followed. He stopped suddenly and turned back to her. "You'd better be worth it."

Mariah fought a smile. It was hard. "Oh, I am." That was when she caught the flicker of desire in his intense gaze.

He finally pushed open the door. "Time will tell." He motioned for her to go ahead of him. She walked out, feeling his gaze and that of every man in the crew on her.

Shane came up beside her. "Everyone, listen up. Sorry about the delay this morning, but there's going to be a few changes you need to know about before we start." He glanced at Mariah. "This is Mariah Easton. She's been hired to act as Paradise's project manager." There were murmurs and groans in the group. "I'm still the crew boss, and you'll answer to me, but Mariah will take over in the office with ordering, deliveries and keeping us on schedule. So mind your manners and cooperate with her." He glanced at her. "You have anything to add?"

Mariah had a lot to say, but she wasn't about to fight with Shane in front of the crew. "No, not right now."

He turned back to the men. "Okay, let's get to work."

She returned to the trailer, praying for strength to survive this job. A hundred times she'd asked herself why she'd agreed to take on this difficult assignment…and Shane Hunter. He'd dumped her once in high school. He broke her heart and it had taken years to get over him. Now she was leaving herself wide open for hurt and being dragged into this ridiculous, decades-old feud.

Mariah picked up the phone. First thing she needed was a desk. There was no way she was sharing Shane's.

She glanced at the stack of papers on top. Her gaze continued around the makeshift office to the drafting table, piled high with blueprints. How did they find anything?

In the empty corner she decided there was room to put a small desk. And it was far enough away from Shane's that maybe they could stay out of each other's way.

"Already calling Daddy to complain?"

She glanced over her shoulder to find Shane had come back inside. "Let's be clear about something. I don't go running to anyone."

"No, well, he came running to you. Guess he needs you to spy on the big bad Hunter."

Mariah ignored him as she spoke into the receiver. "Yes, I've taken the job, but I'll need a desk." She glanced around the messy room with the overflowing trash cans and stacks of empty pizza boxes and grimaced. "And a cleaning crew. This place is a pigsty." She hung up and looked at Shane.

"As you can see, I don't have a problem getting what I want." She walked toward him. "So be warned, Shane. I'm not the insecure girl you remember." It was a lie. "I worked with construction crews who chewed up female project managers and spit them out like a bad taste. I survived and did my job and did it well. Now we can work together or against each other. I'd prefer we work as a team. It will make our jobs easier." She raised an eyebrow. "And if it looks like we're getting along, it will drive my father crazy."

* * *

By noon Shane wanted to get good and drunk, but he needed a clear head. So he drove into town for lunch and some down time instead. When he walked into the town's favorite hang out, the Good Time Café, he found his brother Nate already seated at the counter.

"Hey, bro, what brings you into town on a weekday?"

Shane sat on the next stool. "The trailer is being cleaned."

Nate's eyes narrowed. "Say again."

"The new project manager is having the trailer cleaned. She said it's a pigsty."

"Well, that part is true—whoa, you said *she*. As in a woman project manager?"

Shane nodded.

"Oh, boy."

"It only gets worse," Shane began. "The project manager is Mariah Easton."

His brother made a whistling sound. "Are you talking about the girl you had the hots for in high school? Kurt Easton's daughter?"

Shane nodded twice.

"Oh, man." His eyes widened. "She still pretty?"

"I didn't notice."

Nate grabbed his brother's wrist. "I'm just checking for a pulse. You must have died, because that's the only way you wouldn't notice a woman."

Shane jerked away. "Stop it. Like I had time to check her out."

"You didn't notice all that wild red hair and big green eyes. Those long, long legs…"

Shane didn't want to hear any more. "Hey, didn't you marry a gorgeous blonde about six months ago? I believe her name is Tori. Soon to be the mother of your child."

Nate smiled. "And I love my wife, but I also remember back when you walked around all goofy about that girl. I thought I'd have to buy you a bib because you drooled so much."

"I wasn't that bad." Was he? "Besides, that was years ago," Shane insisted, trying not to remember the time when he'd had no choice but to give her up. "Now, she's just a pain in my…side."

Nate frowned. "Are you afraid that she'll try to undermine your job?"

Shane shrugged. "What else can I think? She's Kurt Easton's daughter."

Chapter Two

"I need the lumber delivery by noon, Mr. Harris," Mariah said into the phone at her desk. Her first morning, and already she'd had to deal with half a dozen problems and it wasn't even nine o'clock.

"No can do, lady," the local supplier said. "My driver won't be able to get the load there until three."

Mariah took a silent breath, not wanting to let him know her frustration. "That means my men will be standing around. It will put us behind schedule."

"That happens in this business. Just sit tight, Jess will be there as soon as possible."

"I don't have time to sit anywhere, nor does my crew. You give me no alternative, Mr. Grant, but to discontinue our business arrangement."

She heard his soft curse. "You can't do that. We have a contract."

"Which you broke when you didn't deliver on time," she informed him. "In fact, the lumber in question was due two days ago." Why hadn't Shane dealt with this problem before now? "That leaves me no choice but to give our business to another company."

"I want to talk with Shane."

Mariah was used to distributors who wanted to deal with a man. "Sorry, he's busy with the crew. Mr. Grant, if we're going to continue our association, you'll be dealing with me, Mariah Easton. I'm the project manager."

The man murmured another curse.

"And you've got until twelve noon today to make the delivery."

"How am I supposed to do that when I don't have a driver?"

"Strap the lumber to your back, just get it here." She slammed down the receiver. What was wrong with her? She never behaved like this. Of course, she'd never had to work with an ex-boyfriend, either. She drew a long breath and closed her eyes. When she finally opened them she saw Shane standing by the door.

"Just what the hell is going on?" he demanded.

He looked like a soft-drink-ad model in his faded jeans and crepe sole boots. The little residue of perspiration on his dark T-shirt that covered his muscular chest only added to his sex appeal.

"I asked what's going on," he repeated.

Great, things were getting worse. "Maybe I should be asking you that." She held out the supply order from the local lumberyard. "This delivery is two days late."

"So I'll call Jerry. He's been having some trouble finding a driver." He went to the phone.

"Mr. Grant and I talked already. I informed him that if the delivery isn't made by noon, then he's broken the contract with the project and will be replaced."

Shane gripped the order form in his hand. So Mariah had jumped into her new job with both feet. She'd started yesterday by having a cleaning crew go over the trailer. Then a desk and file cabinet had been brought in at quitting time. All he'd asked was that nothing in his area be touched, then he'd left and headed to the local bar with some of the guys.

At five-thirty this morning he'd walked into the trailer to the smell of coffee…and Mariah. Dressed in creased khaki pants and a wine-colored blouse, even her work boots didn't take away from her femininity. Her long auburn hair was pulled back from her heart-shaped face and braided, making her green eyes look large and alluring. That was when he'd decided it would be best to get out of the there. So he went to work with the crew.

Now he was trying to hold it together. "Jerry gave us the best price for this project. He's also the only local supplier. I know it sets us back…a little, but I can find other work for the crew."

"It's not good business."

She wasn't giving an inch on this. "This isn't Phoenix, Mariah. Haven is a small town. This project is supposed to bring jobs and revenue to the area. That won't be true if we take our business to Tucson."

"We won't make any money if this project comes to a standstill. I can't back down on this, Shane."

"Can't or won't?"

He met her stubborn look, but soon realized he couldn't intimidate her at all.

"Like I said, Jerry's got until noon," she answered.

Shane moved in closer. He was really ticked off. How dare she come in here and start rearranging things before even asking about the situation? She had certainly changed from the timid girl he'd known in high school. The girl who wouldn't speak or even smile at him for months. Finally he had gotten her to talk to him. He could still recall their first kiss. Her shy response…

"You need to bend a little, Ms. Easton."

"You need to remember this is business, Mr. Hunter, not a popularity contest."

She was driving him crazy. He couldn't decide if he wanted to shake her, or kiss her. He sucked in a breath. Man, he was in trouble. "I've got to go. If you need me, call my cell." He walked out, slamming the door behind him.

* * *

Two hours later Mariah still couldn't concentrate on work. Shane's words kept playing in her mind. She'd never admit it, but he might have been right. Maybe she should have worked things out with Jerry Grant. What Shane didn't understand was that being a woman, she couldn't be soft. Not in this business, and not if she wanted to run this project successfully. If she didn't have the respect and cooperation of their suppliers, she'd never earn respect from the crew.

The door opened and her father walked in holding his cell phone to his ear. At fifty-five, Kurt Easton, the town councilman/businessman was an imposing figure dressed in his dark suit. He acknowledged her with a nod as he continued to talk. Mariah was used to this. Although he tried to be a caring father, he'd always been obsessed with his business ventures and trying to make a name for himself.

He'd come from poor beginnings and always blamed his poverty on the Hunters. Mariah and her younger brother, Rich, had been raised by a man who carried years of bitterness.

Her father closed his phone. "Where the hell is Hunter?"

"He said he was working with the crew."

"I thought that's why I brought you in. To keep an eye on him."

She tried to brush aside the hurt. "I thought you brought me in because I'm good at my job."

"You also need to watch Shane Hunter. He can't be trusted. The site's already been vandalized twice."

She stood and stared into her father's green eyes that were so like hers, hoping that was all she'd inherited from him. "And tell me why destroying *his* property would be the best thing for *his* company?"

Her father backed off with a shrug. "He's a Hunter."

"And I told you when I took this job that I wasn't getting involved in this crazy feud. What went on years ago has nothing to do with Shane, his mother, his brother, Nate or sister, Emily."

"How can you say that when you know Nathan Hunter cheated your grandfather James out of land, and stole the love of his life?"

Mariah had heard the story many times over the years. James Easton had been in love with Catherine Summers. Before he'd been shipped out to fight in World War II, he'd asked his friend, Nathan, to look out for Catherine. Instead, the two fell in love.

"If you continue badgering me, Dad," Mariah continued. "I'll have to resign."

Her father stiffened, then his expression softened. "Okay, just make sure everything is on the up and up. I have too much invested in this project."

"If there are any problems, I'll let you and your partners know."

Just then she heard a commotion outside. "Excuse me, Dad."

She walked to the door, opened it and saw a large flatbed truck loaded down with lumber coming up the road. So her warning had been taken seriously. All her excitement disappeared when the vehicle stopped, the driver's door swung open and Shane jumped down from the cab and marched toward her.

"You wanted the lumber delivered before noon." He checked his watch. "I believe we have five minutes to spare." He grinned at her as he handed her the supply order. "Now I'm going to lunch."

Twenty minutes later Shane climbed the steps to his garage apartment behind his mother's house. He didn't have any appetite for lunch. That was good, since he didn't have any food in the place. He hadn't exactly had an opportunity to shop lately. Hell, with the hours he'd been putting in at the site, he hadn't found much time to do anything.

Shane opened the door to the limited space he'd called home since his newly married brother, Nate, moved to the Hunter family ranch six months ago. Since all his funds were tied up in his business and this project, getting his own place would have to wait.

There was a living room and kitchen combination where a small rust-colored sofa and a large leather recliner faced the entertainment center that housed his one extravagance, a flat screen television and stereo. Two stools were arranged under the short counter that served as the dining area. A narrow hall led to a bath and his bedroom, where he knew his bed hadn't been made in weeks.

His thoughts turned to Mariah. Not two full days on the job and already she was giving him problems. How was she supposed to help the project go smoothly if they couldn't get along? Why hadn't she come to him about the lumber delivery?

Well, he'd shown her, all right. He ignored the sour feeling in his stomach as he dropped his keys on the counter and opened the refrigerator. Inside was a six-pack of beer, a half gallon of milk with a week-old expiration date. He poured it out in the sink and placed the empty container in the trash.

"I guess I'll have another food group." He opened the bread drawer and smiled on finding his stash of Twinkies. He pulled out two and immediately ripped the cellophane off one and took a huge bite.

Just then there was a knock on the door and he finished off the other half of the cake as he went to greet his mother, who was holding a basket of clean laundry.

"Don't tell me that's your lunch."

"Hello, Mom." He took the basket from the slender woman. "And what's wrong with what I'm eating?"

She flashed her piercing blue eyes at him. "Don't get me started." She sighed. "At least come down to the house and fix a sandwich. You work too hard to be skipping meals."

"Mom, I appreciate your help with the laundry, but I can feed myself."

"I didn't do your laundry. I only took your clothes out of the dryer so I could use it."

Betty Hunter tried to act tough, but she still worried about her three adult kids. Now that her oldest son, Nate, was happily married and living out at the ranch, and her daughter, Emily, had moved to L.A., she'd been concentrating all her attention on him.

"Sorry. It won't happen again." Shane took the basket and put it on the sofa.

"That's what you said the last time." She glanced around the apartment. "Now that you have a project manager, you should be able to have a personal life. By the way, how is Mariah?"

"What did Nate do? Rush over to the house to tell you?"

"Nate never said a word. You know news travels fast in a small town. Quit avoiding the question, how is Mariah? She was such a sweet girl."

"Mom, you're talking about Kurt Easton's daughter. He only brought her here to spy on me. He'll do anything to get me off the Paradise project."

"If I remember correctly she used to be pretty smitten with you, and you were crazy about her, too."

"High school was a long time ago," he said quickly.

"And we never should have been together in the first place. We were young and foolish."

"That was a rough time for all of us, especially for you and Emily," his mother said. "You were both too young to lose your father."

When Ed Hunter died suddenly, life had changed for the family. They'd lost everything, including the Double H Ranch. They had to move into town. His mother went back to teaching and Nate came back from Phoenix and took a job in the sheriff's department to help support the nearly bankrupt family.

Shane could still remember the whispers among his so-called friends at school. He hadn't wanted anyone's pity, especially not his girlfriend's.

His mother smiled. "We had some lean years, but we all pulled through."

"I'd like to think so, but it's hard when you have Kurt Easton around to tell you that you're no good."

"Most people don't listen to him. Look at what you and Nate have accomplished—your brother bought the ranch back and is making quite a name for himself with his wood carvings. You've started a construction business and won the bid on a huge project." She smiled. "If I haven't told you lately, son, I'm so proud of you. You can't allow one person's opinion to wear you down."

"Easton's hard to ignore."

"If you're referring to Mariah, she was always such a pretty girl with those big green eyes."

Shane shot her a warning glance. "Mother."

"Okay, I'll stop. But only if you stop worrying about Kurt Easton. His partners hired Hunter Construction because you are the best. It's true he holds a grudge against all the Hunters, but that has nothing to do with you."

"Nothing?" Shane raised an eyebrow. "The man threatens me every opportunity he gets. What exactly did Grandpa Nathan do to set him off?" Shane had heard so many variations of the story he never knew what to believe.

"It was a long time ago and all the parties involved are gone," His mother said. "Unfortunately Kurt continues to keep the bitterness alive."

"Just tell me Grandpa didn't swindle the Easton's out of land?"

"No! Nathan Hunter was a fair and honest man. His only sin was that he fell in love. James Easton and Nathan Hunter were as close as brothers for most of their lives. When James went to serve in World War II, he asked your grandfather to look out for his sweetheart, Catherine Summer.

"Over the next two years, they spent a lot of time together and… Well…one thing lead to another. When James returned, he got angry, and said that Catherine had agreed to marry him. She denied any such promise. Terrible words were exchanged and their friendship ended. James Easton carried his bitterness until his death. It all should have ended then, but Kurt has continued on with his father's grudge."

"And Easton won't quit until he destroys me."

"Then don't let him," his mother stressed. "I know over the years he's given Nate some problems. But to most people in town the Hunter-Easton feud is old news."

Betty sighed. "The one I feel sorry for is Mariah," she said. "Kurt has put the poor girl in a difficult position."

Shane thought back to this morning and her refusal to give an inch. "I don't think you have anything to worry about, Mariah can handle things."

Surprisingly, his mother smiled. "Good for her." She walked to the door.

"Whoa, whose side are you on?"

"Yours. But when it comes to women you've had it far too easy. It's about time there's someone who will make you work for what you want."

The next morning Mariah pressed her fingers against her temples, trying to relieve the headache she'd had since getting out of bed that morning. She shook out two pain pills from the bottle, tossed them in her mouth and swallowed some coffee, hoping the caffeine would make the medication work faster. She hoped Shane wouldn't show up for at least another hour.

She walked back to her desk just as the door swung

open and the man in question walked in. Dressed in his usual work clothes—navy T-shirt and jeans—he looked too good for that early in the morning.

"Morning," he murmured as he strolled to his desk.

"Good morning," she returned as she watched him go through the mail.

"Is this all there is?"

"Except for the invoices, I have those," she said.

"Why? You didn't think I wanted to see how much money is going out?"

She had to concede he was right. "In past jobs I've always handled paying the invoices."

"Go ahead and pay them, but I still want to see them to make sure we're not being overcharged."

"That's my job."

He shot her a glare. "Everything on this project is my job," he said. "That includes yours."

"Are you saying that you don't trust me?"

"Why should I? Your father didn't want me on this project. He lost that battle, but the next thing I know you show up."

Mariah refused to give him the satisfaction of seeing her upset. "You knew there was going to be a project manager. And I'm more than qualified."

Shane folded his arms across his chest. "Your being Kurt Easton's daughter makes me wonder if you're in cahoots with him to get rid of me?"

That did it. "How dare you accuse me of trying to

jeopardize a project," she said, fighting back. "I would never do that."

"Not even for your father?"

She felt as if he'd struck her. She marched over to his side. He was tall and broad, but she didn't let him intimidate her or stop her. She'd faced down a lot tougher men than him.

"Let's get something straight, Shane Hunter. If you ever accuse me of mismanagement again, you better have solid proof, because nobody tarnishes my professional reputation."

Seeing the hurt on Mariah's face, Shane felt like a jerk. It brought back memories of another time he had hurt her. She hadn't deserved it then and didn't now. She hadn't done anything but her job. He just wasn't crazy about her being here.

"Okay. Okay. I may have stepped over the line. But believe me, your father has been riding my case since I was awarded this job. I suppose you can understand why I'm suspicious."

"I guess I understand, but I don't have to like it." She jammed her hands on her hips. "And we still have to find a way to work together, because I don't have the energy to come in here every morning and spar with you."

He couldn't help but smile. "Sure gets the blood going, though, doesn't it?"

She started to grin, and quickly masked it. "Yes, but we need trust and respect between us."

Shane wasn't sure he was there yet. Was it because they had a past together? Was it because she was Easton's daughter? Or was it because he realized he was still attracted to her? Okay, maybe it was a little of all of the above. "I think that will take time."

"Time is something we don't have. We're behind schedule by two weeks. And that doesn't allow for rain delays and—"

Just then the foreman walked in. "What is it, Rod?" Shane asked.

"We got trouble. There was another break-in during the night."

"The hell you say." Shane grabbed a hard hat and followed Rod out of the trailer with Mariah close on his heels. They made their way to the chain-link-fenced area where wood and tools were held. Graffiti had been sprayed on the plywood sheets. Vile, disgusting words had been written on the four-by-eight sheets. Several boxes of nails had been dumped around the area.

"Is anything missing?" Shane asked.

"Not as far as I can see," Rod said. "But we haven't had a chance to take inventory."

"I'll do it," Mariah said as she looked at Rod. "Why don't you get the crews started so there are no more delays?"

The foreman nodded, then walked away.

Shane was surprised at Mariah's suggestion. "I can't leave you to clean up this mess."

"Why? You think it's beneath me? I've gotten my hands dirty before. I would appreciate it if you'd send Jason and Mike to help me out. Later, you and I need to talk about better security. The drive-by patrol doesn't seem to be doing the trick."

"I agree with you on that one," Shane said.

Her green eyes rounded. "Well, that's a start. We finally agree on something."

Around midnight Shane yawned as he slowed his truck at the turnoff to the site. He couldn't sleep, so he decided to do something useful. Until they got the new security in place, he was going to do some checking of his own. Anything was better than lying in bed unable to sleep. Nothing he'd done could turn off his thoughts about Mariah. She just kept popping into his head. Those big green eyes, her full mouth and all that wild hair had him wound tight. She'd been pretty in high school, but she was a knockout now.

And it would be suicide to start up something with her.

This was business and if he wanted Hunter Construction to fly, he had to pay Nate back the start-up money he'd loaned him over two years ago. That meant he had to keep focused on the project. Any thoughts of Mariah had to be about how hard she'd worked on the clean-up today; how she hadn't complained; and how she'd made a detailed list of every item by quitting time.

They both decided whoever vandalized the site wasn't a pro. More like teenagers or someone just wanting to make trouble for Shane. His first thought was that Easton might be behind the incidents, but he couldn't see the town councilman taking a chance on dirtying his hands with such an amateurish stunt.

The truck's bad suspension jarred Shane in his seat. One hundred yards before he reached the trailer, he turned off his lights and parked. If anyone was trespassing, he wanted to surprise them.

That was when he saw the faint light in the trailer. Someone was inside. He got out of his truck and ran across the field. Silently he inserted his key, quietly pushed open the door and saw the person's shadow on the wall. He reached out, grabbed the intruder and pinned him against the wall.

It didn't take Shane long to realize that he was pressed against a soft body, a soft body with breasts.

"Let go of me," Mariah demanded as she wiggled against him.

Desire shot through him and he fought to control his response. "Then you better tell me what the hell you're doing here in the middle of the night."

Chapter Three

Mariah couldn't get air into her lungs with Shane pressed against her. His face was so close she could feel his breath on her cheek. She smelled his fresh, male scent that had traces of soap and a lot of just…Shane. It brought back memories of a different time, a time when they'd shared long, slow kisses. A time when his mere touch could give her such pleasure.

She shook away the thoughts and managed to suck in needed oxygen. "Get off me." She pushed at him, but he didn't budge.

"I asked, what are you doing here?"

"I'm working," she said.

He finally released her. "Why so late?"

"I came back tonight to get some things done." She

pushed past him. "You've been neglecting a lot of the paperwork, Shane. I'm surprised the crew ever got paid."

"I have an accounting service do payroll."

"But who checks the timecards to make sure they're correct? I've been wading through your mess, trying to get things straightened out." And she hadn't wanted to sit at home and listen to her father trash Shane the entire night. "I didn't realize it was so late."

"You don't have any business here at this hour."

"I have as much as you do," she shot back.

Shane then ran a hand over his face. "Okay. Okay. Do you think we could try and get through five minutes without arguing?"

She shrugged. "Do you?"

"Ah, hell." He marched to the other side of the trailer as if trying to calm down. Finally he looked at her. "Mariah, we have to find a way to work together. This might not matter to you, but if Paradise Estates doesn't finish on schedule, I might as well kiss my construction business goodbye."

"Why do you think I'm trying to destroy you? I have as much at stake as you do." It hurt her that he distrusted her. She fought to keep the emotion out of her voice. "I have a reputation to uphold, too, Shane. You have to stop attacking me at every turn."

"I'm trying. But when I walked in here yesterday and saw you..." He came back to her. "My God, Mariah, it's been years. I couldn't help think about how it was between us." He reached out to touch her cheek.

She pulled away again. "You must have different memories from me. I only remember the kiss-off." In all fairness to Shane, she'd known he'd had a rough time after his father's death. All she had wanted was to be there for him, but he hadn't wanted her. She'd been crushed when he'd told her he couldn't see her any longer. What had devastated her was that he'd had time to spend with several other girls in school.

"So, I was a selfish bastard," he offered. "I was a randy teenage boy. Besides, your father didn't want us to be together, anyway."

Mariah shrugged. "That never stopped us. We'd found ways to see each other." She knew she was baiting him, but she liked seeing his reaction. "I would drive out to the ranch."

"And you took foolish chances," he reminded her.

She couldn't stop the memories. She would park behind the barn, and he'd run out to meet her. She'd barely be out of her car before he had pulled her into his arms and kiss her.

She glanced at Shane. The look in his eyes told her he was remembering, too. "You never asked me to stop," she accused.

Suddenly he drew her close again. "How could I? You were every teenage boy's fantasy."

Her pulse raced. Hearing his confession, feeling his

hard body pressed to hers, she hadn't the strength to pull away. She hated her weakness for this man.

Shanc's head lowered to hers, and she eagerly met his mouth. She whimpered as her lips parted and his tongue pushed inside. Sliding her hands up his chest, she circled his neck. All the feelings she'd buried so long ago suddenly surfaced. Every dream she'd had about being with Shane again hadn't compared to this. Desire spiraled through her body, exploding through her senses, making her feel a hunger she'd never known.

Then, all too soon, it ended.

With a curse Shane released her and turned away. The rejection was excruciating for Mariah. Once again she'd let Shane Hunter hurt her.

His gaze met hers. "That was a mistake. The last thing we need is this kind of complication."

She took a shaky breath, trying to slow her pulse. "I agree. I shouldn't have baited you."

He nodded. "How's this going to make for a working relationship?"

"If you think I'm going to resign, you're wrong. I don't give up that easily."

"Then we better set some guidelines."

She didn't like him being so calm and controlled over what just happened. "How about the first one is you keeping your hands to yourself? Let's keep this a business relationship—nothing more."

He started to speak, then nodded. "And how about you not coming out here alone in the middle of the night?"

She nodded. "And you tell me when a supplier has a problem with delivery. I'm not a tyrant. Something can be worked out. It's important to me, too, that we use local suppliers for this project."

"How about if you don't run home every night and tell Daddy every detail of the day? I don't want to give him any ammunition to use against me."

She frowned. "I don't discuss our business with anyone. But I do live with my parents…at least temporarily."

He cocked an eyebrow. "Are you looking for a place of your own?"

She wasn't going to tell him about the run-ins with her father. "I have my *own* apartment in Phoenix. I haven't lived with my parents since before college. I would like a temporary place while I'm here, but that's impossible to find without having to sign a lease."

"If you're not looking for anything special, I know of a studio apartment."

"I'm interested."

He nodded. "Then meet me at the Good Time Café for breakfast."

"I don't have time for breakfast."

"You will tomorrow." He picked up her purse and handed it to her. "And now we're both going home to bed." She tensed when he placed his hand against her back and guided her to the door. "Tomorrow we'll put our heads together and figure out how to do our jobs."

"I like the sound of that."

"And I mean it, Mariah, no more coming out here alone late at night. It's too dangerous."

"Would it help if I told you I know karate?" When he frowned, she went on, "Maybe if someone was here it would keep the vandals away."

"Or they could come after you." He escorted her to the door. "The only way you get to be out here is if I'm with you. We have to start working together. Agreed?"

When he looked at her with those blue eyes, she couldn't deny him what he wanted.

"Agreed," she said, knowing she was in big trouble.

At six-thirty the next morning, Mariah walked into the Good Time Café. She wasn't surprised that the fifties-style diner was crowded. The place had always been a popular spot in Haven and that obviously hadn't changed. She glanced around at the red vinyl booths that lined the windows. A young waitress was rushing through the group of tables refilling mugs as the jukebox played an old song by the Supremes, "Baby Love."

She recognized several of the crew as she continued to search the room. Finally she found her man seated at the counter. A jolt of awareness hit her. One curious kiss did not make Shane Hunter *her* man. They couldn't afford to let anything else happen between them. They needed to keep all their concentration on the project.

She started across the room toward Shane. He was engrossed in conversation with the man next to him and he suddenly threw back his head and laughed. It had been a long time since Mariah had seen Shane this relaxed. She knew that working with her wasn't easy for him.

Shane swung around on the chrome-and-vinyl stool. The smile faded a bit as he got up and came to greet her. "Good, you made it."

"I figured if I didn't show, you'd come and get me."

"You got that right." He took her arm and guided her to the counter. "Mariah, do you remember my brother, Nate?"

With a smile she offered her hand. "I hear it's Sheriff Hunter now."

The tall, handsome man in his khaki uniform stood as he took her hand. "Not for much longer. I'm retiring in another a few months. Nice to see you again, Mariah. It's been a few years."

She was surprised that the former football star remembered her. "Yes it has. I've been living in the Phoenix area."

"Shane tells me you're doing a good job of cleaning up his act."

"Well, what can I say? He needs it." She sat down on the empty stool next to him.

Nate laughed, reminding her so much of his younger brother. "Good luck. The family gave up on him years ago."

"Hey, I'm right here," Shane called out. "Nate, don't you have a job to do or a wife to go home to?"

"Not at the moment." Smiling, he turned back to Mariah. "I think things are a lot more interesting right here."

Shane hated how Nate was acting. Smiling at her and being so sickeningly sweet. The man was married. Just then a customer vacated the stool on the other side of Mariah, and Shane sat down.

"Well, we have business to discuss, so get lost," he said, hating his sudden possessiveness over Mariah.

Mariah looked at him. "We don't start work until seven. Since I'm here, how about some food?"

"You want breakfast, I'll get you breakfast," Shane said as he waved and got the attention of the waitress.

She hurried to the counter. "What can I get for you, Shane? More coffee?"

He smiled back at the teenager. "That would be nice, Lisa, and Mariah, here, would like the breakfast special."

He glanced at Mariah and found she wasn't happy that he'd ordered for her. She turned to the waitress. "I would like eggs scrambled hard and wheat toast."

After Lisa left, Nate and Mariah went back to their conversation, completely ignoring him. Seeing his brother's sappy grin, he realized this was payback for all the times he'd flirted with Tori. Nate was wasting his time, he wasn't interested in rekindling a relationship with his high school sweetheart. All he was interested in was them working amicably together.

Shane caught Mariah's reflection in the mirror against the wall. His gaze locked on her expressive emerald-green eyes, then lowered to her full mouth. His heart skipped as he glanced away. So what if the woman was a turn-on. That didn't mean he had to do anything about it, did it?

Just then Nate's radio went off. He stood up to check the message. "Well, looks like I'm needed to help keep the peace. It was nice seeing you again, Mariah. I hope I get the chance to introduce you to my wife, Tori."

The waitress brought Mariah her breakfast. "I'd like that."

"Well, I'm out of here. 'Bye, bro," Nate said as he smacked Shane on the back, then walked to the door in time to hold it for the customer coming in.

Shane groaned as Betty Hunter stood at the doorway. His fifty-five-year-old mom showed off her trim figure in her gray running suit.

Smiling, she made her way toward them. "Hello, Shane." She kissed her son, then turned to Mariah.

"Well, if it isn't Mariah Easton." Betty gripped both of the younger woman's hands. "It's been a long time."

"Hello, Mrs. Hunter. It's nice to see you again." Mariah's gaze went over the older woman. "You look wonderful."

"Thank you, I try to stay in shape." She glanced at Shane then back to Mariah. "I hear that you're working with Shane."

"That's right. I'm the project manager."

Betty smiled. "Isn't that nice."

He could see the wheels turning in his mother's head. "Mom, what are you doing downtown this early?"

"I got bored and decided to change my running route."

"And you stopped by here because..." Shane nudged her.

"Well, I saw Nate's patrol car outside and I wanted to tell him that Emily is coming home this weekend."

Shane was surprised. "She's flying in from L.A.? Just for the weekend?"

None of the family had been happy that Emily had chosen to work in the movie industry. Not when that meant she'd relocated to Los Angeles after college. "Maybe she's come to her senses and is moving home."

Betty frowned. "No. She's not giving up on her career. But she said she's got some good news for us. So Tori and I are planning a barbecue at the Double H Saturday."

Shane knew his sister leaned toward the dramatic. Everything had to be a big production. "Why can't she just tell us at the house?" Shane tried to squelch his irritation. He'd planned on putting in some extra time at the site during the weekend. "Besides, Nate always ropes me into some work at the ranch."

"Not this time. It's strictly a party." His mother glanced toward the kitchen and waved to Sam Price, the owner of the café. "I'm going to invite Sam and ask him to bring his coleslaw." His mother looked at Mariah. "Oh, and Mariah, we'd love to have you to come, too."

Caught by surprise, Mariah stopped with a forkful of eggs midway to her mouth. "Oh, Mrs. Hunter, thank you, but I can't intrude on family."

"Nonsense, you could never intrude. And I'm sure Shane would love to show off the work he's done on the ranch house. Please, I know for a fact that Emily is bringing someone with her."

Great, now she was getting coupled with Shane. She couldn't look at him, but she wondered how he was handling this. "Thank you, I'll think about it."

"Mom will get her way," Shane began. "So you might as well agree to come now."

Mariah laid down her fork. She couldn't swallow anything past the lump in her throat. She smiled at Mrs. Hunter. "Okay, I'll drive out."

"There's no need," Shane spoke up again. "I'll take you."

Before Mariah could argue, Sam came out of the kitchen and greeted Betty.

"Hey, stranger," he said to Shane. "I haven't seen you in a while."

"I've been sitting right here for the past thirty minutes."

"I guess I wasn't looking." Sam turned to Mariah. "I'd rather look at my pretty customer. Hi, Mariah. I heard you were back in town."

"Hi, Sam." She smiled at the older man with the thinning gray hair and stocky build. He hadn't changed in years. "You look just the same."

"Holding my own. It's harder to keep up with the kids. They don't all like my taste in music."

Mariah knew the old jukebox only had fifties and sixties classic rock 'n' roll records. Sam had probably taught most boys in Haven how to dance. "Well, I'm still a fan."

"Good. I also hear you've got the tough job of keeping this guy in line."

Shane glanced over his shoulder. "Is there a sign on my back that says Pick on Me?"

The group laughed. "We've never needed a sign," Sam said, and folded his arms. "So what brings you in this morning?"

"Breakfast," Shane offered.

"Well, I've got to go," Betty announced as she touched Sam's arm and walked away.

Shane had thought for a long time that there might be feelings between his mom and Sam. Not that they ever acted on them. But it was obvious to everyone else the two cared about each other.

After Betty left, Sam turned his attention back to Shane. "What really brings you in?"

"Mariah wants to rent your room upstairs."

Sam shrugged. "I haven't even been up there since Tori moved out."

"So we'll clean it up."

Sam's gaze met Mariah's. "It isn't much."

"I don't need much," she said. "It's just temporary until the project is finished."

Sam went through the double doors to the kitchen and seconds later came back with a key. "You show it to her, Shane. I can't leave right now."

"Come on," Shane said as he got up.

Mariah grabbed a piece of toast and took a long sip of her coffee. "A girl can starve hanging around you."

Shane called to the waitress to box up the food. "You can take it back to the site." He took Mariah's hand and pulled her though the kitchen, then out the back and up the steps.

When Shane opened the door, Mariah tried not to react, but it was hard. Although the place was tidy, it was dark and dingy. And small. "You didn't lie when you said it wasn't much." She walked into the tiny bathroom with only the barest necessities.

"You have to look at the positives," Shane said.

She cocked an eyebrow. "And those would be…"

"You're a lot closer to the site."

That was true. Her parents lived on the other side of

town. "There isn't exactly a lot of rush hour traffic in Haven."

"You wouldn't have to keep defending me to your father."

"What makes you think I do?"

He shrugged. "Okay, you can avoid having to report in to him everyday."

That was the best reason. She glanced at the double bed with the thin cotton coverlet. "I'm going to miss my mother's cooking."

Shane followed her to kitchen area. "Sam serves a pretty good dinner every night. It's pretty close to Mom's."

She looked at the one cracked tile counter. "Doesn't look like I have enough room to have a party." She sighed. "That could be the deal breaker."

His eyes met hers. A lock of dark hair fell across his forehead. Damn, he was sexy. And damn, if he didn't know it.

"I guess you'll have to invite fewer people," he suggested. "Myself, I'm more into the smaller, more-intimate get-togethers."

Mariah was insane to even think about taking this place, even worse, thinking about Shane being the one here with her. But she couldn't stop herself as she reached out and took the key from him. "I'm not going to have time to have any *kind* of parties."

"All work and no play makes Mariah a dull girl."

"Sorry, that's who I am."

There was that sexy glint again. "I guess we'll have to see if we can't change that."

By Saturday Mariah was happy she'd survived her first week on the job. Thanks to Shane's change of attitude, she was starting to build a rapport with the crew. But her hardest task had been to move out of her parents' home.

Kurt Easton wasn't the easiest man to live with under normal circumstances, but now that she'd accepted the position on Paradise Estates, she couldn't handle his third-degree interrogations anymore.

Years ago her father had an alcohol problem. It had been one of the reasons she'd gone away to college. She loved her family, but she had to leave for her own sake. The guilt had plagued Mariah, knowing her young brother, Rich, was left to deal with the effects of the disease. Even though her father, who had reluctantly given up alcohol after being diagnosed with diabetes, had been in recovery for five years, that didn't mean everything was perfect within the family. Since her return to Haven, her brother hadn't hid his resentment toward her. Maybe her moving out was a good idea.

With a satisfied sigh, Mariah glanced around her new home. In the past three days she'd painted the dingy walls of the tiny apartment yellow and bought new curtains for the lone window. Bright towels and rugs added needed color to the bathroom.

None of this took time away from her job. While she

restructured the office, Shane worked with the men, trying to make up time lost. They'd also hired a security company out of Tucson. There would be two men living at the site, and they would install more floodlights.

Mariah took one last check in the mirror on the closet door. It was early May, and although it was a warm spring day, she'd donned a pair of jeans and a teal-colored blouse. Instead of the work boots she wore every day, she'd put on her favorite pair of western, black hand-tooled Tony Lamas.

She grabbed a sweater when she heard the knock on the door. Shane. She blew out a long breath and let him in.

Not waiting to be invited inside, Shane crossed the threshold wearing a pair of new jeans that hugged him in all the right places and a blue western shirt accentuated his broad shoulders. He smiled. "Wow. Look at this place."

A little disappointed that he hadn't noticed her first, she murmured, "It's just a little paint."

His gaze finally returned to her, and he smiled. "You look…nice, too."

"Thanks." She went to the counter and picked up the potted rosebush with blooming rich-pink-colored buds.

"What do you have there?"

"Just a housewarming gift. I heard Tori is into gardening."

Shane looked at the patent tag. "Victoria's Gift." His gaze went to Mariah's. For a long time he didn't say a word as his piercing blue eyes mesmerized her. "Be careful, you might lose your image as a tough guy."

She smiled, knowing he was trying to get a rise out of her. "You're not as bright as I thought, Shane Hunter. I'm not a guy."

"Oh, I've noticed. More than I should."

A thrill raced through her as she fought to keep from blushing.

"Maybe we should get something straight before we go out to the Double H," he finally said.

"What's that?"

"My family. Since we're going out together, they're going to assume we're a couple. And the more we deny it, the more it will add fuel to the fire."

Mariah felt the disappointment to her bones. "So you don't want me to go? Okay, I understand." She handed him the rose. "Just give this to Tori and tell her I had to work."

"Whoa. Whoa. Who said anything about not wanting you to go?" His gaze met hers. "I just wanted to warn you, and make a suggestion."

She was almost afraid to ask. "And what would that be?"

"To act like we're a couple."

Mariah was speechless. Was he crazy? Was he trying to break her heart again? She saw his charming smile. He was acting so smug, as if she'd just fall into his arms. Well, two could play at pretending....

Chapter Four

On the way to the ranch, Shane could feel Mariah's tension from across the truck cab. And he had to say he couldn't blame her. This was getting complicated. As much as he'd tried not to get involved, she'd inched back into his life.

He didn't need a woman right now, especially not Mariah Easton. There was no way they could ever have a future together, no matter how beautiful and sexy she was. So after today, there wouldn't be any more socializing.

Shane drove under the wrought-iron archway that announced the entrance to the Double H Ranch. His chest swelled with pride as he glanced around at all the recent improvements to the place. Just six months ago

Nate had managed to buy back the land and since had worked tirelessly at rebuilding the old homestead that had been in the Hunter family for nearly one hundred years.

He had done his share, too, spending endless weekends and evenings restoring the house, updating the kitchen before his brother brought his bride back from San Francisco.

He parked in front of the newly painted yellow house with white shutters. Hanging baskets of colorful flowers adorned the large gingerbread-woodwork-trimmed porch.

"Oh, I've always loved this house." Mariah turned to him and smiled. "I heard you've done a lot of work on it."

He could barely manage his next breath. "How did you know?"

She shrugged. "Rod mentioned it." Her green gaze locked with his. "I'm glad that your family got the ranch back."

He nodded, knowing she meant it. Mariah wasn't like her father. She'd never harbored ill will against anyone, not even a Hunter. But Kurt Easton expected nothing less than total loyalty from his daughter. And she would give it.

"Well, it's Nate who owns it," he said. "He inherited the Hunters' talent for ranching. I'll stick to building."

"Your grandfather also built this home for his family. I'd say that's where you got your talent."

Shane wished her praise didn't mean so much to him. Before he could say anything, the front door opened and Tori came out to greet them. She was still slender, barely showing, even though she was five months pregnant.

By the time they got out of the truck, Nate, Sam and his mother were swarming around them, too.

"I'm so glad you could make it," Betty told Mariah, then embraced her.

"It was nice of you to invite me," Mariah said.

Shane took the plant from the back. "Tori, this is Mariah. Mariah, Tori."

Mariah found she was nervous as she took the rosebush from Shane and gave it to Tori.

"It's lovely. Thank you, Mariah." The petite blonde smiled. "I just hope I can keep it alive."

The group broke out in laughter as another couple came around the side of the house. Mariah recognized Emily Hunter, tall and shapely, with dark-brown hair and those deep-blue eyes. She was dressed in a blue blouse, creased jeans and boots. The sandy-haired man with her was also handsome, and definitely city bred. Dressed in khaki chinos and a yellow polo shirt, he walked across the uneven ground as if afraid of soiling his loafers. There was no doubt Emily's beau had never been on a ranch.

"So you got tired of L.A. and decided to come home?" Shane teased.

"Now, why would I want to come home so my brothers can boss me around?" She came closer, her eyes, so like her brother's, sparkled.

"Damn, if I don't miss giving you a bad time." He grabbed her in a big hug. "Good to have you home, Em."

"It's good to be home." She pulled away. "Even if it's only for the weekend."

Shane glanced past his sister. "Who's the guy?"

"Oh, Jason, I'm sorry." She brought him closer and did the introductions.

Jason smiled and enthusiastically held out his hand. "It's great to meet you, Shane. Emily has talked about her family so much I feel I know all of you."

Shane shook his hand, wondering if this guy was Em's boyfriend. He brought Mariah to his side. "Em, you remember Mariah Easton. She's back working on the Paradise project with me. Mariah, my sister, Emily, and her friend, Jason."

Emily gave her brother a sly smile as if asking if something was going on.

After they shook hands, Nate came up to the group. "Okay, sis, everyone is here. Now can you tell us your news?"

Emily grinned. Immediately Shane shot a glance down at her left hand, expecting to see an engagement ring. But it was bare. He felt relieved.

"Well, I brought Jason home with me because he

wanted to look around the ranch. He's checking out locations."

"Locations for what?"

"Jason is in films. Jason Michaels Productions." She looked about to burst. "I sold my manuscript, *Hunter's Haven*."

There was a gasp from their mother. "Oh, Emily, that's wonderful. I know how hard you've worked on it."

"Way to go, sis." Shane hugged her again, remembering that for years Emily had done extensive research on the Hunters settling of the area.

Next Nate and Tori came with their congratulations. "I hope you had a lawyer look over the contract," Nate said.

She nodded. "My agent handled everything," she explained as she waved him off. "That's not the best part. Jason's company has brought *Hunter's Haven* movie rights."

The group looked stunned as Emily went through the details. "He wants to begin production in the next few months." She looked at Nate. "He thinks the Double H Ranch is the perfect location to film my story."

An hour later the women were in the kitchen preparing food while the men were watching Nate barbecue the steaks on the patio.

Mariah moved around the beautiful kitchen amazed

at Shane's handiwork. He had designed the functional space to perfection, from the abundance of maple cabinets and granite countertops, including a work island with an extra sink.

Mariah recalled the tour of the rest of the house, the restoration of the hardwood floors and fireplace. All the bathrooms had been redone in natural-colored travertine.

The man had such talent. She'd known that years ago. At one time, he'd had dreams of studying architecture. They'd both had so many dreams back then. Their biggest was wanting to be together. They planned to go to the same college so her father couldn't keep them apart. Then Ed Hunter had died and everything changed. Shane's world had crumbled and he'd turned away from her.

Mariah suddenly heard her name called. She glanced at Tori, feeling heat rush to her face. "Sorry. I guess you caught me daydreaming."

Nate's wife smiled as she came up to her and whispered, "With these handsome Hunter men that's pretty easy to do."

Mariah started to deny any such foolishness but couldn't. "What do you need me to do?" she asked instead.

"We're just about ready, so why don't you start carrying the food out to the patio. Nate said the steaks were almost done."

Mariah nodded and picked up bowls of potato salad

and coleslaw and walked through the French doors to the redwood deck. Deep laughter greeted her as she found Shane, Nate, Sam and Jason standing around the biggest barbecue grill she'd ever seen.

Shane had his back to her. The man looked good from any angle. His western shirt stretched over his broad shoulders, then tapered down to fit his narrow waist. Indigo-colored jeans hugged his slim hips and long muscular legs. He turned around, then rushed to take one of the bowls from her hand.

"Thanks," she said.

He gave her one of those Shane smiles, causing her breath to catch and her heart to skip a beat. Darn the man. She'd known that their spending a "date" together wouldn't be a good idea.

"Hey, lighten up," he told her when she tensed. "We're a couple, remember? I'm supposed to be attentive to you."

"I don't think it's necessary that you try so hard."

He set the bowls on the glass-topped table, then took her by the arm and walked her across the deck so they would be alone. "What's the fun in that?"

She knew she was being foolish. What would it hurt to play along? "I don't like being on display. Every time you come near me, your entire family stops everything to watch us."

His mouth twitched. "You think so?"

Just then his mother, sister and Tori carried the rest of the food outside. "Then maybe we should give them something to talk about." His head lowered, and his lips touched hers in a sweet, tender kiss. Mariah knew she should put a stop to this but couldn't seem to manage it. She grabbed his forearms and held on as he took a teasing nibble from her lower lip. She gasped in sheer pleasure.

Suddenly Nate's voice brought her back to reality. "Hey, you two, break it up. It's time to eat."

Shane broke off the kiss and winked at her, then escorted her to the table. "Boy, am I hungry," Shane called as he took the seat next to his stunned companion.

Later in the afternoon Shane walked toward the barn in search of Mariah. He knew he was playing with fire to spend any more time alone with her, especially after he'd kissed her in front of his family.

He told himself it was all for show. Just a game to keep his mother off his back. That was until his mouth touched hers. Then everything and everybody seemed to disappear and there was only Mariah.

He pushed away the lingering feelings. It had been stupid. After their encounter last week in the trailer, hadn't he sworn never to touch her again? She was dangerous. And he didn't need to be tempted any more than he already was. They had to work together for the next three months.

But damn, if she didn't make him want to risk it all.

Inside the barn, his eyes worked to adjust to the dim

light as he walked down the concrete aisle. At the end he found Mariah next to Gypsy's stall, crooning and petting the pregnant Appaloosa mare. She looked relaxed, carefree and beautiful.

And he wanted her. Badly.

She turned toward him, and her smile faded, even though he could feel that the sexual awareness sparking between them was as hot as ever.

Her eyes locked with his. "Shane—"

He ignored her hesitation and reached for her, drawing her into his arms. "If you're going to say you don't want me to kiss you, then I'll have to call you a liar." He drew her body against his. Her softness nearly drove him crazy.

"We shouldn't do this," she protested weakly.

He shook his head. "Liar," he said, just as his mouth captured hers. He would deal with the consequences tomorrow. Right now all he wanted was the feel of her in his arms. When she opened her mouth, he slipped inside to hear her sweet moan. Her arms went up around his neck and she deepened the kiss.

With a groan he brought her against his evident desire, as a hunger he'd never known coursed through him. His hand went to her breast, finding her hard nipple through her blouse.

She gasped and he pulled back, but his gaze never left hers. "You want me to stop?" His fingers continued to work the tight bud.

She shivered and tugged his mouth back down to meet hers. The need intensified, and he didn't want to do anything but feel as Mariah ran her hands over his chest. Her silken touch made him burn. He pushed her back against the stall and aligned his body with hers. They fit together perfectly.

"Feel what you do to me, Mariah." His breathing was ragged. His mouth took hers again in another hungry, needy kiss. He held her tightly as he stroked her, tasted her honeyed sweetness.

Suddenly Shane heard Nate calling his name. He broke off in time to see his brother walk into the barn. With a curse, he glanced down at Mariah. Seeing her flushed face and swollen mouth, he felt protective as he hugged her close. "Easy, babe, it's okay."

Nate gave a sly smile as he came toward them. "Sorry to interrupt."

"Then why did you?" Shane asked as he tried to gather his composure.

"It's just a heads up, bro. In about a minute Emily and her city-slicker producer will be out here. They're going to ride out to the homestead. Sis wants you to go with them." He glanced at Mariah and smiled again. "And so do I. If they decide to use the Double H for the movie location, they'll need to do some reconstruction on the old cabin. And before I agree, I want you to think about doing the restoration."

"Okay, we'll ride out there." He felt Mariah stiffen.

Nate nodded. "I need some help rounding up the horses." Without waiting, he took off.

Once they were alone, he pulled a resistant Mariah back into his arms. "I'm sorry Nate interrupted us."

She didn't look at him. "Maybe it was for the best. Look, I don't need to go riding. I'll just stay here and keep Tori company."

She started to walk away, but he stopped her. "My mom will keep Tori company. I'd like you to go along." Even knowing they were getting too involved, he still meant it. "I don't want our time together to end. I promise I'll keep my hands to myself."

She teased him with a half smile. "It's not just your hands I'm worried about."

"Okay, I won't kiss you." He reached for her. "But till then I'll need something to tide me over." Then his mouth captured hers in one last kiss.

Mariah knew she was crazy. Crazy about Shane Hunter.

As she walked her horse along the trail, she realized nothing had changed during the years away from Haven. Every man she'd tried to have a relationship with, she'd compared to Shane. And they'd never measured up. But how could she let herself have feelings for the man, when she was afraid to let herself trust him? She could never love a man she couldn't trust.

Not to mention the fact that her father would probably disown her. No matter how absurd Kurt Easton's reasons were for hating the Hunters, he wasn't about to change. And where did that leave her? She would have to pick between the two men.

As if Shane knew she was thinking about him, he glanced over his shoulder and winked at her. Her pulse began to race as she remembered the kisses they'd shared in the barn.

Finally they arrived at the Hunters' original homestead. The structures were nearly gone. The two-room rough log cabin was missing part of the roof, but the floor was intact. There was a barn and the remnants of a corral.

Shane climbed off his horse and went to help Mariah down. As much as he tried to concentrate on the business of filming *Hunter's Haven* here, he could only think about her. The way she felt in his arms and how much he wanted to hold her again. He shook away the thought and climbed the single step to the porch as he began to size up the place. Although there wasn't much left, the hundred-year-old cabin's foundation had held up through the generations.

"This is great," Jason said. "This is exactly what I'd pictured when I read Emily's manuscript. Of course, the cabin had a roof and all the walls."

"I think the roof blew away about twenty years ago," Nate said. "Remember, Shane? Dad tore away the rest so we wouldn't get hurt."

Shane checked out the stout framework. "Yeah, I remember. I also remember helping to clear out the mess."

Nate came up to him. "What do you think, Shane? Can we restore it?"

"Yes we could, but I guess the bigger question is *should* we restore it." He glanced at Mariah who was standing beside Emily. "This is Hunter family history. It almost feels irreverent to disturb this place."

Nate nodded. Shane knew what it had cost his brother to get the Double H back in the family. How he'd saved every extra penny he'd earned, and when the rundown ranch went on auction last summer, he'd managed to buy it and bring it back into the Hunter family.

Nate turned to the producer. "Jason. I think I'm going to renege on my offer," he said. Emily's gasp was audible. "But I'm going to make you another one. How about I waive any location fees you were going to pay me, and instead of you using the original homestead, we use the money to build a replica just over the rise toward the north?"

Jason looked at Emily and she nodded. "Sounds good. Could I see the area?"

Nate smiled. "Sure." He started for the horses.

Shane called to his brother. "If you don't mind, Mariah and I are going to head back to the house." He watched his brother, his sister and friend ride off, then turned to Mariah and smiled. "Alone at last."

"You could have gone. I know my way back."

"I didn't want to go with them. I wanted to talk with you."

"I don't think we should talk about anything but the project. It's safer that way."

"What about you and me?"

"There is no you and me, Shane." She shook her head for emphasis. "We're working together. Nothing more."

"So those kisses meant nothing?" His eyes narrowed. "You clinging to me, letting my hands caress your body was nothing?"

She shivered and fought the feelings he evoked with every ounce of her willpower.

"I won't deny that we're attracted to each other."

"Attracted? Hell, sweetheart, we set off so many sparks we almost burned down the barn."

"So what are you trying to prove, Shane? That I still have feelings for you?"

He didn't know how to answer her bluntness. "It is still there between us."

"Just because you're a good kisser, doesn't mean that I'm going to throw myself at your feet. We aren't in high school any longer," she told him as she clenched her fists. "There's too much in our past for us ever to have a future. And the sooner you realize that, Shane Hunter, the better it will be for all of us."

Chapter Five

Shane drew Mariah into his arms, reveling in her inviting warmth as her body molded against his. Need sprang through him when her mouth opened willingly to his kiss. Desire coiled tighter as she took everything he gave, demanding more.

When he lowered her to the bed, the mattress gave under their weight, the sheets cool against their heated skins, doing nothing to halt the fever. For so long he'd been unable to think about anything but Mariah. He had wanted her for so long.

"Shane…make love to me," she whispered as she arched against him.

"My pleasure," he said as he pulled her beneath him…

Then suddenly there was a ringing sound. He tried to push it away, but it grew louder and Mariah's voice began to fade.

No! He cried, don't leave me. With a gasp, he jerked up in bed, realizing it had all been a dream, and the ringing sound was the phone.

He grabbed the receiver. "This better be good," he growled, breathing hard.

"How about another break-in at the site?" Mariah said.

His body was still humming as he glanced at the bedside clock—2:05 a.m. "Mariah?"

"The security guard couldn't reach you so he called me. You must sleep like the dead."

He ran his fingers through his hair, trying to pull himself together. "Well, I'm awake now. I'll meet you at the site in thirty minutes."

Mariah had just gotten out of her truck when Shane's black pickup came to a skidding halt next to hers. He jumped out, buttoning his shirt, flashing a glimpse of his hard, flat stomach before he tucked the tails into his jeans.

A rush of sensations shot through her body when she saw his mussed hair and that sleepy sexy look on his face. Had he turned off his phone because he didn't want to be disturbed? Had he been with a woman? She recalled his breathless voice when he finally answered the phone. She didn't want to care, but she did.

He gave her a curt nod. "Where's Roger?"

"I haven't seen him, I just got here myself. But I'm going to find out." She marched off through the muddy field toward the row of newly framed units.

Shane caught up to her. "Did he tell you anything over the phone? Did they catch the guy?"

Mariah stopped. "Look, Shane. I know as much as you do. If you hadn't been so occupied you could have answered your phone and you could have asked Roger yourself." She started to walk away but he stopped her.

"What the hell are you talking about? I wasn't occupied with anything but sleep."

"If you say so." She hated being jealous. What if he *was* with another woman? She pushed away the thought. That was his business.

The overhead security lights showed off his slow, easy smile. "You thought I was with a woman?"

She stiffened. "Who you spend time with doesn't matter to me. Unless it interferes with work." This time she pulled away and didn't stop until she found the two security guards, Roger Shields and Jerry Turner, standing outside one of the framed structures.

"Sorry to call you out, Mariah," Roger said. He was a stocky-built retired marine who still wore a buzz cut.

"I thought we had them," the other guard, Jerry, said. He had a slighter build but was an expert in the martial arts.

"What's the damage?" Shane asked as he came up behind her.

"They sprayed this entire structure with graffiti," Roger told him. "Jerry and I went after them, and we finally caught one, and that's when we saw the flames coming from the other structure. We released him and ran to put out the fire."

"Gasoline," Shane said. "I can smell it."

"Oh, God," Mariah said. "This is bad. Did you call the fire department?"

Roger shook his head as he glanced at Shane. "We got the fire out before it spread. These kids are novices, but I'm afraid that if we don't stop them, someone's going to get hurt. I smelled alcohol on the one kid. I just wish I could've gotten the ski mask off his face."

"Did you see a vehicle?" Shane asked.

"No, but they ran off across the field. They must have had a four-wheel-drive vehicle to get through the rough terrain."

Shane stepped inside the structure, shone his flashlight along the sheets of graffiti-sprayed plywood. "Damn. Who's doing this to us?" he murmured as he moved the light from the foul words.

"I didn't call the sheriff, Shane. But maybe you should. Even if these are kids, they're playing a dangerous game."

"I'll talk to my brother in the morning. We just don't want the word to get out about this kind of trouble. It could label Paradise Estates as jinxed."

"That isn't your biggest problem," the security guard said. "Whoever's doing this is serious. This place could have burned down tonight."

He blew out a long breath in frustration. "What do you suggest I do?"

"Call the sheriff," Roger said, and walked away.

Shane knew he was right. He just couldn't imagine anyone in Haven doing something like this. Was it teenagers playing some sort of prank? He didn't care who was responsible for this trouble, he just wanted it to stop.

He headed off to the house next door and found Mariah inside. The strong smell of gasoline lingered.

"Man, this is bad."

"Not so bad." Mariah held the flashlight on the stack of wood just outside the corner of the structure. "If we get rid of the plywood, we'll get rid of the smell." She looked at him. "Go get your truck and we'll load it up and make a trip to the dump. The stench should be gone by tomorrow. No one will know."

He was surprised. "What about your father? Shouldn't you tell him about this?"

Mariah shook her head. "He hired me to handle things. And I feel this is the best way to deal with the problem."

He relaxed. Maybe they could be a team. "I couldn't agree with you more."

"But, Shane, we can't keep letting this happen. We

were lucky tonight, but we can't keep taking these hits."
She stiffened. "I'm sure as heck not going to let some
troubled kids destroy my project."

Shane couldn't help but smile at her fierceness and
her protectiveness. She was on his side. "That's my
girl."

She frowned. "I'm not your girl. I'm your project
manager."

"Can't you be both?" He went to reach for her.

"Don't you have enough women as it is?"

He liked that she cared enough to be jealous. "I told
you, I was sleeping."

She didn't look convinced. "Or maybe you were just
distracted." She marched off toward the trailer. Shane
quickly followed her, wanting to make her believe him.
He grabbed her by the arm to slow her progress.

She wasn't happy. "Shane, let go of me." She strug-
gled to break his hold.

"Just as soon as I tell you a few things."

She stopped fighting him and folded her arms across
her chest. "Okay, talk."

"First off all, I wasn't with anyone tonight or any
other night since you came back to town. Do you really
think so little of me that I could be with you, kiss you
the way I did, then take another woman to my bed?"

She blinked at his bluntness.

"It took me so long to answer the phone because I
was asleep…and dreaming about you." He blew out a

long breath. "And, sweetheart, it was definitely *R* rated, and it would have gone to *X* if the phone hadn't wakened me."

He took a step closer. "I'm kind of glad you did interrupt me, because I'd like us to go that step together." He kissed the tip of her nose and made himself walk away. He knew she still wasn't ready to trust him. And he wanted that trust more than anything.

It was after eight o'clock the next evening when an exhausted Mariah walked into her small apartment. After they'd finish the cleanup at the site last night, Shane had followed her home. Then, after a few hours sleep, she was back at the site, only to discover Shane and Nate were waiting for her.

Together they talked unofficially with the sheriff about the incident the previous night. Shane's brother promised to increase the patrols around the site, hoping to keep the intruders away. After Nate left, Shane didn't go to work with the crew. He'd stayed in the trailer and spent the morning on the phone, doing the paperwork he so dreaded.

It was nice that *he* could work, because he distracted her so much that she couldn't get hers done. Thank goodness he'd left at five, so she'd finally been able to get the payroll finished.

Now home, Mariah stripped out of her work clothes and climbed into the shower, letting the warm water soothe her body longer than usual. Tonight she wanted nothing more than some food, a little television and a lot of sleep.

She got out of the shower and dressed in fresh jeans and a white cotton T-shirt. She left her hair piled on top of her head and walked out to her tiny kitchen area. She didn't have much in the food department and was thinking about ordering something from the Pizza Palace when there was a knock on the door.

She wasn't expecting anyone. She pulled open the door and saw Shane on her doorstep standing under the glow of the porch light. He was dressed in a starched cream-colored western shirt and creased jeans.

"Shane. What are you doing here?"

His smile faded a little. "Wow, you sure know how to make a guy feel welcome." Without waiting for an invitation, he stepped past her and into her small apartment.

"Look, Shane. I'm really tired tonight. I was just going to order some food—"

"Good, you haven't eaten. I'd like to take you out for dinner."

This wasn't what she needed. It had been bad enough that he knew she'd been jealous. "I really don't want to get dressed up and go out."

His blue-eyed gaze traveled over her body, and she felt her heart soar. "You look perfect just the way you are. Besides, we're not going far."

She opened her mouth to protest but couldn't, especially when he reached for her hand and held it in his.

"Oh, all right, I am hungry." And I'm crazy. "But I don't want to be out late."

"No problem."

She nodded, then went to slip on a pair of sandals and hurried into the bathroom. She ran a brush through her hair and applied some lipstick, hating the fact that she was looking forward to spending the evening with Shane. After a few calming breaths, she walked out.

Shane smiled. "Good, you took your hair down." He tucked her arm through his, and they walked out and down the steps. Instead of getting into his truck, he surprised her when he escorted her to the café's back-door. He took her through the vacant kitchen with only a dim light over the grill, then through the doors to the main part of the café.

"Oh, Shane." The restaurant was closed, so the room was dark, shades pulled for privacy. Rows of flickering candles lined the counter, throwing off a soft glow. One of the tables was covered by a white cloth adorned with two place settings and a vase of roses in the center. In the background the jukebox played the Righteous Brothers singing "Unchained Melody."

She swung around to face him. "You did this?"

"I did most of it, but Sam cooked the food. I wanted to take you someplace special. "You've put in a lot of hours. I just want you to know how much I appreciate it." He took a step closer. "And I wanted to take you someplace we could talk without outsiders bothering us."

Even though she was thrilled with the idea, she knew one of the outsiders he was talking about was her father.

"Hey, why the frown?" Shane took her hand. "There's no worrying about work tonight. Tonight is to help you relax. It's been a rough week."

Shane took her hand and drew her to the small dance floor. Once in his arms, Mariah forgot every argument about why she shouldn't be doing this as he drew her against him. She couldn't resist leaning into his solid strength, and for the first time in a long time she let herself get lost in the moment.

All too soon the music ended. Shane pulled back slightly, reluctant to let her go just yet. He wanted to keep her like this forever. "Do you still love that song?"

She looked up at him with those big green eyes. "You remembered?"

He nodded. "I also remember you cried when we saw the movie *Ghost*." She'd come out to the ranch and they'd watched the video together.

She smiled. "You weren't supposed to notice that."

"It was a little hard not to, when your tears were all over my shirt," he said, and quickly added, "Not that I minded. A guy wants any excuse to hold his girl in his arms."

"That wasn't all you wanted to do," she murmured.

Oh, he remembered, all right. How he'd ached to touch her. That feeling had only intensified over the years. "What can I say? I was a teenage boy."

Her smile faded. "Yeah, you had quite a reputation." She pulled away, and he let her go, knowing the moment had passed.

"How about a glass of wine?" He went to the ice bucket on the counter and filled two glasses. He held one out to her.

She took a sip. "This might put me to sleep."

"I'll take my chances. Besides, I'm hoping it will relax you enough so you can enjoy yourself."

She sniffed the air. "If that's Sam's lasagna, I know I'm going to enjoy myself."

"So, I have to feed you to get your attention?"

She cocked an eyebrow and he nearly kissed her. "You can have my attention, as long as I can eat."

He guided her to the table. "Your wish is my command." He went into the kitchen and came out with two plates of lasagna, then returned with a basket of bread.

Shane took the seat across from her. He couldn't help but smile as he watched her dig into her food. He smiled. It was a start.

Chapter Six

The following Monday morning Mariah arrived at the site at 6:00 a.m. and found that Shane was already at his desk. He gave her a curt nod as he continued to talk on the phone.

So it was business as usual.

When he finally hung up he came across the room to her desk.

"Hi," he said as his gaze lingered on her. He toyed with a pink message slip.

"Hi," she returned as she nodded to the paper in his hand. "Is there a problem?"

He blinked. "Yeah, Ben Combs called me last night. He crashed his motorcycle over the weekend."

She gasped. The carpenter had been one of the first to welcome her. "Is he all right?"

"He's pretty banged up and broke his arm. He won't be able to work for at least six weeks."

"Then we'll need to find someone to replace him," she said, feeling heartless to be thinking about the work schedule. But it was necessary.

"You're right. We can't afford to lose any ground, so I hired Chuck Harper. I worked with him last summer. He'll be here by eight."

"Good." Mariah studied the man's name on the paper. She couldn't look at Shane, not without remembering their meal and dance they shared Friday night at the café. Deep down it made her angry that he hadn't tried to call her or come by her apartment over the weekend. She hadn't heard a word from him all weekend. Was he playing with her? Or, since she hadn't given in easily, maybe he'd lost interest. Memories of years ago flooded back when Shane had suddenly disappeared from her life. She wouldn't leave herself open for that kind of hurt again.

She didn't need any attention from Shane Hunter. She only had to work with the man. She wasn't being paid to notice how sexy he looked in his fitted jeans and T-shirt or remember how his smile and laughter sent a warm tingle through her.

No! She didn't need to think about any of that.

Best thing to do was keep her distance. So for the

rest of the morning Shane worked quietly on his side of the trailer while she worked on hers.

She would be able to do that if her father hadn't called her four times to ask her frivolous questions. When another call came in, she realized he was more and more agitated, and sometimes his conversation hadn't made any sense.

Mariah finally insisted he stop phoning her. With the promise she'd stop by and fill him in on how things were going that evening when she got home, she hung up. Mariah closed her eyes, remembering years back when her father had been drinking. She remembered the rough times that had nearly destroyed her family and had kept her away. She thought those days were in the past. But were they? She glanced across the trailer to find Shane watching her.

"Is something wrong?" he asked.

Her emotions were too close to the surface to hide. She called on her last ounce of courage and stood.

"Nothing a little lunch wouldn't help solve. Can I bring you back anything?" She prayed that Shane wouldn't offer to go with her.

"If it's not too much trouble, I'll take a cheeseburger and fries." He reached for his wallet.

Mariah refused to take the money. "I'll get it. You paid for breakfast the other day."

"Whatever."

Mariah almost made it to the door when Shane stopped her. She sucked in a breath.

"If I'm not here when you get back, I'm out with the crew," he said. "Just call me on the radio." For a moment their eyes met, and silence stretched between them, as did the sexual awareness. He spoke first. "You sure you're okay?"

Mariah managed to nod at his honest concern. He made it so easy for her to lean on him. But could she risk her heart with him again?

Twenty minutes later Mariah walked into the Good Time Café. The place was crowded with people, but the soft sound of music muffled the noisy conversations. She looked past the booths and saw several high school kids grouped at the jukebox. She noticed a tall, lanky boy with too-long, blond hair. Her brother, Rich.

She smiled. She hadn't seen much of Rich since she'd moved out. Maybe she could talk him into having lunch.

She made her way through the tables to the postage-size dance floor in front of the vintage jukebox. "Hi, Rich."

He swung around, and his smile faded when he recognized her. "Mariah. Hi."

"What are you doing out of school?"

"We only had half a day." He slipped his hands into his jeans pockets. "So I'm just hanging out."

She glanced at the other boys. Rich made no move to make introductions, but she was more concerned at their reluctance to make eye contact with her. But then she had no right to question her brother's friends. "If you're out of school, why don't you come out to the site? I'll show you around."

His eyes grew large. "No! Why would I want to do that?" He glanced at his friends. "We've already got plans. So we got to go." They started to walk away, but Mariah stopped her brother while the others headed for the door.

"Rich, I was hoping we could spend some time together. If not today, maybe another time."

"Suddenly you want to play big sister? You moved out of our house and in with the enemy."

How could he think that about her? "What are you talking about?"

"You're awful chummy with the Hunters."

"I work with Shane."

"Is that where you were going two weeks ago when he was at your apartment?"

Had her brother come by the day she went to the ranch? "No, we went out to the Double H. Mrs. Hunter invited me."

"Does Dad know?"

"I don't have to report to Dad about my whereabouts." So her father's prejudices had been passed on to the next generation. "You know that Shane Hunter hasn't done anything wrong. Whatever happened between our grandfathers sixty years ago should be dead and buried. Don't let Dad poison your mind."

He stiffened. "All I know is that we Eastons have to stick together. We're family. You're the one who's forgotten her loyalties."

That hurt. "It was Dad who brought me in for this job. There are no enemies here. Just a stupid feud that needs to end."

"How can you say that? Mariah, they stole our land. And I'm not going to listen to you defend them."

"I'm not defending anyone. Please, Rich. Let's talk about this." She reached for him, but he pulled away and rushed out of café.

She watched through the window as her brother climbed into the new extended-cab truck their father had bought him and sped off. How could she help him if he wouldn't listen to her?

"Mariah?"

She turned around to see Nate.

"Is everything okay?"

"Oh, Nate. I'm sorry. I guess you caught me daydreaming."

He frowned. "I was talking about your brother. Was Rich giving you trouble?"

She wasn't about to air her family troubles in public. She forced a smile. "Just teenage stuff."

The sheriff didn't look convinced as he followed her

to an empty stool at the counter. "Are you sure that's all it is?"

Did she have to worry about Rich now? "Why? Is there something I should know?"

Nate shrugged. "Sam's had some minor trouble with Rich and his friends, but so far he's handled it."

Mariah was embarrassed. She knew Sam had strict rules for all the kids who came in the café. If they didn't follow the rules they were banned from the place. "Is there something more I should know about?"

"I've caught him ditching school a few times. He gives me attitude sometimes. So, I've talked with your mother. She promised me she'd talk to him. Most of the time kids outgrow these things." Nate's eyes twinkled. "Shane and I turned out pretty well."

"Your brother still has his moments," she said, realizing she was acting as if they still were a couple.

Nate took the vacant stool next to her. "You both looked pretty cozy that day out at the ranch. You two having trouble so soon?"

It was time to end the game. "We only looked cozy so your mother would stop playing matchmaker. It was all for show. I'm just working with Shane. There's nothing between us."

A big grin spread across Nate's handsome face. "It's a good thing Mom wasn't in the barn to see that hot kiss. She'd be planning a wedding right this minute."

* * *

Shane checked his watch. It was after one o'clock. Where was Mariah? She usually never took a lunch break, and now she'd been gone for over an hour and he couldn't find her. He knew she'd been upset about something when she'd come into work, but he'd let her go off on her own, anyway. He should have gone with her.

The door to the trailer opened and his heart skipped a beat and then suddenly accelerated as his eyes took her in. He hadn't had much chance to get a good look at her this morning. Not when it took everything in him to ignore her. It had nearly killed him, but it was what she said she wanted. A purely professional relationship.

Mariah didn't want him to notice how well she filled out a pair of jeans, making him wonder just what her legs looked like underneath. Her hair was pulled back into a tight braid, but he'd remembered how the loose, wild curls felt in his hands.

He shook off his wayward thoughts. "Where have you been?"

She went to his desk and dropped the sack on it. "Lunch."

"That was over an hour ago. I've been trying to reach you on your cell phone."

"So, I'm back now," she said irritably. "What was the major problem you couldn't handle?"

"I didn't say I couldn't handle it. I just wanted to be able to reach you."

"I had some personal business, okay? I thought you could manage an hour or so without me."

He noticed a sadness in her eyes that her curt tone wouldn't disguise. "Mariah, what's wrong?"

"Nothing."

When she marched past his desk, he reached out and grabbed her by the arm. "Don't give me that. What happened?"

"Oh, suddenly you're concerned, when this morning you couldn't even look at me."

He cocked an eyebrow. "Isn't that what you wanted?"

"What I want is honesty, Shane. I don't want to play games. You lied to me about your mother's matchmaking."

Who had she been talking to? "My mother has been matchmaking with Nate and me since we turned twenty-one."

"So the couple act at the barbecue was for her benefit?" Her eyes looked bleak. "How about the dinner at Sam's? Was that for you Mom's benefit, or was it just to see how long it would take you to get to the tough project manager? Flirt with her, kiss her into surrendering, and then on Monday morning treat her like you don't know her."

He felt like a heel. "No, Mariah, it wasn't like that."

He reached for her but she jerked away. "I swear. I thought I was doing what you wanted." He raked a hand through his hair.

Tears flooded her eyes.

He moved closer. "All right, I kissed you at the barbecue. The kiss on the patio might have been for my family, but the one in the barn was strictly because I couldn't stop myself. I knew that I deceived you to get you to go to the ranch, but I thought once you were in my arms…"

"That I'd succumb to your charms," she added for him.

He fought the smile but lost. "A guy can always hope." He quickly sobered. "If that were true, why would I back off and give you space? I meant it when I said I care about you. I want another chance."

She shook her head. "Why would I put myself through this again? You pushed me away once before." She shook her head. "That hurt, Shane."

"I was seventeen years old. What I did was prideful and stupid." He reached out and cupped her cheek. "My life was turned upside down when my dad died."

"I know it was, and I wanted to be there for you."

"Oh, Mariah." He took a step closer, but before he could pull her into his arms, the door swung open.

Kurt Easton entered the trailer, looking irritated and angry. Mariah jumped back but Shane refused to let her father intimidate him.

"What do you want, Easton?"

"I want to know why in the hell you aren't working," he said, his words slurred. He swayed as he moved toward the desk. Was he drunk?

"Why aren't you out working the crew?" Easton demanded.

"I'm working here."

"The hell you are. Mariah can run this office. So go pick up a hammer and start pounding, Hunter."

"Dad, please." She went to him. "Shane has a full crew working and we're nearly back on schedule."

"I want him out there." He pointed an accusatory finger.

Shane had had enough. He was about to call one of the other partners to show them this side of Kurt Easton.

Then Mariah took charge.

"Dad, how about I run you home and I'll fill you in on what's going on," she coaxed. "Mom can fix you some lunch."

"I don't have time. This project is behind schedule," her father insisted weakly. He blinked and began to sway. Shane rushed to his side just as he stumbled. "Whoa, Kurt. I think you'd better sit down."

"Get your hands off me, Hunter."

Shane ignored the futile struggle as he easily led Easton to a chair. There wasn't any scent of alcohol, but the man's skin was clammy to the touch and he was sweating profusely. Something wasn't right. "Kurt, are you taking any medication?"

The man tugged at his collar. "That's none of your business."

"I'm sorry, Shane," Mariah said. "I need to get him home."

"Mariah, I don't mean to pry, but has your father been drinking?"

"My dad hasn't been drinking. He is…a diabetic. He didn't want anyone to know."

Shane immediately went to the small refrigerator in the corner, took out a bottle of orange juice and twisted off the cap. He held it out to Easton. "Drink this, Kurt."

"I don't want any." The older man weakly pushed it away.

"Mariah, get your father to drink some. I'll call the paramedics." With Mariah's nod, Shane pulled out his cell phone, punched in 911 and explained the situation to the operator. "They're on their way."

The fire department arrived in ten minutes. While the paramedics worked on Easton, Shane went outside the crowded trailer just as the sheriff's patrol car drove up.

Nate climbed out. "What happened?"

Shane realized he wasn't as steady as he thought. "Kurt Easton started acting confused and disoriented. My guess is it's diabetic shock."

"I didn't know Easton was a diabetic."

"Neither did I. It seems Easton has been keeping his

condition a secret." Shane could think only about Mariah. He wanted to be with her but knew he had to stay away so they could work on her father.

Twenty minutes later Easton was on a gurney and being wheeled to the ambulance. Mariah was behind him, looking pale and frightened.

He went to her. "How is he doing?"

"Dad's better, but they're taking him to the hospital. I have to go with him."

"Of course you do."

More tears formed in her eyes. "Oh, my mother. I need to call her."

"Not to worry, I'll go to the house and bring her to Haven General." He gripped her hands in support. "Just go and be with your father. I'll take care of the rest."

"Thank you." She hurriedly climbed into the back of the ambulance. He watched until they drove off, then he talked to Rod, giving him instructions for the rest of the day.

Shane went to his brother's patrol car. "Can you give me an escort to Easton's house?"

"Sure," Nate said. "Oh, boy. Kurt's going to hate this. The Hunters helping the Eastons through a family crisis."

Shane could care less what Kurt thought. He was only worried about one person. Mariah.

It was nearly three hours later when Mariah came out of her father's cubicle in E.R. Her mother had arrived thirty minutes after the ambulance, and she hadn't left her husband's side since. The doctor had confirmed that her father had diabetes. And Kurt Easton wasn't handling it well.

Mariah wasn't, either, especially when she felt guilty about thinking the worst of her father. That he'd started drinking again. All this time he'd been sick. She drew a long breath and released it. He could have died today if…

She glanced across the waiting room and saw Shane slouched in a plastic chair, his long legs stretched out in front of him. His eyes were closed, his head tilted back against the wall. A warmth rushed through her. He was here for her. She hadn't expected him to stay, and although she hadn't been sure she'd wanted him here, she was very glad he was.

She walked to him and, as if he sensed her presence, he opened those mesmerizing blue eyes and straightened in his chair. "Hi."

"Hi," she answered, finding she was a little breathless. "Shouldn't you be at the site?"

"I'm in touch with Rod." He patted the cell phone in his pocket. "I'm where I want to be. Besides, I can go back later to check out things. How's your father?"

"He's stable. I want to thank you for your quick thinking." She glanced away. "If you hadn't been there…"

He stood and put his arm around her shoulders. "Don't think about it, Mariah. The important thing now is that your dad is going to be okay. And the doctors will get it under control."

"How did you know what to do?"

"My grandfather was a diabetic. There was one time when I was twelve and Papa Nathan acted like that. He was the one who told me about the orange juice. It's very important that your father doesn't skip meals and that he takes his medication."

"Oh, my mother will keep a closer eye on him from now on."

He smiled. "It's going to be fine, Mariah." He drew her against him and she let him.

Around seven o'clock that evening, Mariah returned to the site. Shane's truck was parked beside the trailer. She didn't want to face him again, not when she felt so vulnerable. Not when he'd been so kind and caring with her. And not when he'd made her feel so safe when he'd held her in his arms. She tried to push aside such thoughts, but nothing worked to stifle the memories of his tenderness, his concern today.

Mariah had fought so hard not to lean on him, on anyone. She'd prided herself on her strength and independence. When she was a child, her father had let her down with his drinking, then Shane had abandoned her in another way. His rejection had been just as devastating as her father's actions. Although she'd forgiven both, she still couldn't let down her guard.

A quick glance around the site told her that the crew was already gone for the day. One of the security guards drove by in a golf cart. He greeted her and continued on his tour as she headed up the steps and went into the trailer. Shane was at his desk talking with the foreman. She went to her area and decided to finish up some paperwork.

She found tomorrow's crew schedule on top. After a few minutes Rod came by to inquire about her father, then left.

Suddenly the trailer seemed to shrink, especially when Shane walked over and sat down on the edge of her desk. "Mariah...you didn't need to come back here. I can handle things."

She nodded. "I know, but Dad has to spend the night at the hospital, so I thought I'd just finish up some of this paperwork."

He frowned. "Is he okay?"

"Yes, the doctor just wants to make sure he's stabilized. He's going to have to change his diet and learn to take insulin." She sighed tiredly. She knew it was her mother's life that was going to be difficult.

"What about you?" he said. "You've got a lot on your plate right now. Why don't you take a few days off."

What was he trying to do? "No. I can handle it."

"Mariah, I know you feel guilty about thinking your father was drinking."

"Stop!" She held up a hand. "I don't want to discuss it." She'd never shared that information with anyone, but she realized that somehow Shane knew the family secret.

"How did you know?" she asked after a tense moment of silence.

He was quiet for a moment, then shrugged. "You know small towns, everyone knows everyone's business."

Great! She looked at him. "So now you know life in the Easton household wasn't perfect. In fact, it was pretty rough sometimes." She didn't want his pity.

"Was that the reason you went away to college?"

She nodded.

"Was that also the reason you only came home a handful of times in the past ten years?" Shane asked. "Or was it me?"

She couldn't get into this now. Her emotions were too raw "Don't flatter yourself, Mr. Hunter. I got over you a long time ago," she lied.

He clutched his hand to his heart. "A direct hit."

"Like you care that I left. You were too busy dating every girl in a fifty-mile radius. I doubt you even noticed I'd gone."

"But I did." His voice lowered. "I stopped by your house the day before you were to leave. Your mother answered the door and said you didn't want to see me."

Mariah was shocked. "Mom never told me."

He shrugged. "It was probably for the best. I just didn't want you to go away with hard feelings." His incredible blue gaze locked with hers. "I never meant to hurt you, Mariah. It's just that after Dad died…and we lost the ranch… I had a lot to deal with."

She could see it still bothered him. "I know. We were both so young."

His gaze held hers. "And I cared for you so much."

She swallowed against the dryness in her throat. "And I cared a lot for you, but my father caused so many problems. Going away to college seemed to be the answer at the time…for everything."

Shane took her hand in his. "We're a lot older and hopefully wiser now. I'm glad you're back. And I'm hoping that you'll be staying."

This was too much to deal with. She didn't want him to make her hope again. "Shane, right now I can't think about anything but this project…and my family."

He placed a finger against her lips. "Don't waste your energy arguing, Mariah. You and I have always had something between us. We have since I walked into the school assembly and I saw you for the first time. Man, you took my breath away when you smiled at me."

Shane watched Mariah as her beautiful green eyes widened. He'd blown it years ago. Now was his chance to lay his cards out. "Since we're being honest, Mariah. I want to finish our discussion from earlier."

She suddenly moved away. "I think it's best to leave this alone."

He wasn't going to let her deny what was between them. He went after her. "You said you didn't like me playing hot and cold toward you." He reached for her. "And we both know that whenever we get close it's definitely hot." He drew her into his arms, and his mouth covered hers.

It was a tentative kiss, but one fueled by his building passion and his emotional need for her. He held her tighter as he parted her lips, moved his tongue inside to stroke and tease her until her arms went around his neck and she clung to him.

Mariah was light-headed. She finally relented and let herself sway against him.

"I've wanted to do that since I left you at your door Friday night," he said. "Three times on Saturday I started to call you, and twice on Sunday I got in my truck to drive to your apartment. I only stopped myself because I know you had a lot of other things on your mind."

He traced his finger along her lower lip, and she lost the ability to resist. Such a small touch, but it sent heat through her body, making her ache. He took another teasing nibble from her bottom lip. "Tell me you wanted to see me just as much as I wanted to see you."

It would be a disaster if she told the truth. Yet, she couldn't stop herself. "Yes," she confessed before she surrendered to another kiss.

When he tore his mouth away she found it impossible to draw air into her lungs. "I could do this all night," he told her.

"You're not playing fair, Shane."

He placed tiny kisses along her jaw, sending shivers through her. She was falling fast.

"Just tell me you'll give us another chance," he said.

"Shane, we can't let our feelings get in the way of our jobs."

"You're putting up too many obstacles. We can do the Paradise project and still spend some private time together."

She laughed. "Now I know you're crazy."

His gaze met hers. "Yeah, about you."

NO POSTAGE
NECESSARY
IF MAILED
IN THE
UNITED STATES

BUSINESS REPLY MAIL
FIRST-CLASS MAIL   PERMIT NO. 717-003   BUFFALO, NY

POSTAGE WILL BE PAID BY ADDRESSEE

SILHOUETTE READER SERVICE
3010 WALDEN AVE
PO BOX 1867
BUFFALO NY 14240-9952

Chapter Seven

A few days later Shane had just hung up the phone when Mariah walked into the trailer after lunch. As usual, she'd been to her parents' home to see her dad.

And Shane had missed her like crazy.

Two nights ago she'd asked him not to push a personal relationship, and he hadn't. They both knew that their concentration had to be focused on the project, and Mariah had been working overtime, trying to help her mother deal with her father's diabetes.

"Hi," she said as she went to her desk.

"Hi, yourself." He grinned as she bent over her desk, enjoying the way her jeans fit her shapely legs and round bottom. When she stood up, she turned and glared at him as if she knew what he'd been thinking.

"Don't you think you'll get more work done if you keep your mind on business?" She fought a smile.

"Since you're so good at reading my mind, see if you can guess what I'm going to do now." He crossed the room, reached for her, but she was too quick and avoided his grasp. She glanced toward the door as if someone might walk in at any moment. "Shane, behave."

He did as she asked and backed off. "You're just too tempting."

"Well, try to restrain yourself." She backed away and sat down at her desk. "This is a workplace."

"Then let's continue this tonight. Let's go out to dinner at the steakhouse." He wanted to convince Mariah that they made a good team and pitch to her how they should continue their personal relationship.

"I thought we talked about this. We aren't going to get involved."

"We are involved. I want to spend time with you, Mariah. I want to take you out on a date."

She hesitated, and he knew she was tempted. "I can't. I told my dad I'd come by for dinner tonight."

Great. "How's your dad feeling? Any idea when he'll be returning to work?" Easton had been running his wife and daughter ragged. He thought nothing of summoning Mariah to the house several times during the day and evening.

"I think next week."

As far as Shane was concerned, the one good thing about all this was that Easton had been off *his* back. And that made his job easier. But he also knew how exhausting this ordeal had been for Mariah. "Your dad is one of the project investors. I'd gladly fill him in on how things are progressing here."

Mariah tossed him a skeptical look.

"Okay. Maybe that isn't a good idea." Shane was desperate. "So if you can't do dinner tonight, how about we take off early and have a drink? There's something I'd like to discuss with you."

Although they'd spent a lot of time together at the site, they hadn't been out in public. He wanted them to be a couple.

"Maybe that's not a good idea right now," she hedged.

That hurt. "Well then, tell me when it will be a good idea."

She remained silent.

Maybe she didn't want them to be together. "I guess I misread your signals. I thought you wanted to spend time with me."

"It's not that, Shane," she began. "But you said you'd go slow. We both have responsibilities."

"Not likely I'd forget it, but there's time for other things, Mariah. I thought there might be time for us, but I guess I was wrong." He grabbed his hard hat from the desk and slammed out of the trailer. He headed straight for the framing crew, hoping that pounding some nails would help work off his frustration.

It was after nine o'clock that evening when Mariah pulled her truck up next to the Hunters' garage. She glanced up at the apartment overhead. The light was on. Shane was home.

She drew a shuddering breath. He deserved her honesty, but that could get her hurt. It was safer to tell him they couldn't be together and keep him at a distance. That way she wouldn't get hurt. More important, her father wouldn't get upset. The problem was, she didn't want to let Shane go.

Mariah got out of the cab and climbed the steps. Before losing her nerve, she knocked on the weathered door. The seconds passed like hours as she waited, then the door swung open. Shane appeared dressed in jeans, an opened shirt that exposed his bare chest. She couldn't breathe, let alone speak.

"Mariah, what are you doing here? Did something happen at the site? Don't tell me we had another break-in?"

She shook her head. "I…wanted to talk to you, but if this isn't a good time." Losing her nerve, she started to turn away. He stopped her.

"Mariah, just tell me if your being here has anything to do with the project."

She shook her head.

A slow, sexy smile appeared on his face. "You came to see me?" he breathed, and pulled her into the apartment.

Mariah felt helpless to resist him. It was useless, just like trying to stop her feelings for him.

She nodded as her arms went around his neck. "Just so you know, Shane Hunter, there are a dozen reasons why I shouldn't be here. Why I shouldn't want to start up anything with you."

His mouth swooped down to meet hers, stealing her words, her breath.

"How can we work together?"

"Happily," he whispered, and took a teasing bite from her bottom lip.

She gasped and moved closer, reveling in the feelings Shane created in her. She couldn't stop herself as she raised up and placed her mouth against his. Her tongue teased his lips now, and she was thrilled at the sound of his reaction. He groaned and wrapped his arms around her, crushing her against him.

"Shane," she gasped as he swept her up, walked her to the sofa and sat down with her on his lap. She didn't want to think about anything except loving this man.

"I missed you," he admitted in between kisses. "I can't tell you how glad I am you're here."

"I shouldn't have come. We are playing with fire, Shane. My father…" Her words died out as his hand moved under her shirt to caress her bare skin. "Dad will never accept this, or us."

"Your father isn't here, Mariah. It's just you and me. We're all alone."

Shane's mouth crushed down on hers. He let her know she was the only one he cared about, the only one he wanted. He managed to release her bra, then his fingertips went to work teasing her nipples into hardness. She sucked in a breath as her gaze locked with his; she could see the mirrored desire in his eyes.

Mariah moaned as he sent shivers through her sensitized skin. She gripped his shoulders as a shiver shot through her all the way to her toes.

Then without warning Shane broke off the kiss and tugged her shirt back down but didn't release her. She felt his heart drumming against her chest, both their breathing was ragged.

"Shane…"

He cradled her head to his shoulder. "Just don't say anything. I want you so much I'm about ready to explode. But you aren't ready for this, Mariah. And I care about you too much to take advantage of you."

"I do want you," she said, trying to handle the turmoil racing through her.

"And I want you. But things are going so fast, I think we need to slow down. We haven't even been out on a date."

Shane kissed her on top of her head. She knew he

was right, but that didn't stop her ache for him. "You sure have changed since high school. You were all hands, always trying to get into my bra."

He chuckled. "And all I wanted was to get to first base, but you always fought off my best moves."

Suddenly her own self-doubt threatened to consume her. "I always thought…that was the reason you broke up with me."

When she heard him curse, she tried to move off his lap, but he held her tight.

"Mariah, that was the last reason I broke up with you. I was all messed up when my dad died. But you mattered to me. It's just that my family lost everything—our home, money."

"I understood that. I wanted to be there for you, but you were running around with all those other girls…" This was crazy. They weren't in high school any longer.

He blew out a long breath. "I can't deny I've been with some women, but not nearly as many as my reputation would imply."

Mariah was curled against him, her head pressed to his shoulder. She wanted to believe him. "I should go home."

"No until you hear me out." He cupped her face in his hands. "Make no mistake, Mariah. I wanted you then and I want you now. But if I carried you into my bed and made love to you tonight, I can pretty much bet you would regret it tomorrow morning." He shook his head. "I couldn't stand that. I want more than one night with you." He drew a long breath and released it. "You have a lot on your plate right now. We both do.

"And I have a ways to go before my business is solvent." He cocked an eyebrow. "Having said all that, I can't stop the ache I feel for you. I want you back in my life, Mariah." He raked his fingers through his hair in frustration. "I know we don't have much time apart from the project, but we should be able to handle a date now and then. How do you feel about going out with me?"

"I'd like that, too," she said, feeling a little giddy. "What about my father?"

He held up a hand. "I know Kurt holds a grudge against my family, but, Mariah, this is your life."

She knew that, but her father had been so sick. "Can we not shove it in his face right now? He's having trouble dealing with his illness."

"Lady, I just want to be with you." Shane kissed her thoroughly before he pulled back. "Damn, you're too tempting," he said, and released her. "We need a distraction." He helped her off his lap and stood. "I have something I want you to look at." He led her to the kitchen counter.

"I don't want you to think that I'm only after your sexy little body. I'm crazy about your mind, too." He opened a file. "Would you look over this project for me?"

"You're such a sweet talker, Shane Hunter. You can really turn a girl's head."

His smile widened. "I do my best."

The next morning Shane parked his truck next to Mariah's. Even with the lack of sleep she'd caused him last night, his heart raced with the anticipation of seeing her again. He bounded up the steps, swung open the trailer door and hurried inside. Before he could say anything to the beautiful woman behind the desk, he noticed that two of the crew, Jack and Tom, were standing there.

"Hey, Shane," Jack said. "You working with us today?"

Shane broke eye contact with Mariah and looked at the men. "Someone's got to watch you guys," he said with a grin.

Mariah handed the two carpenters their paychecks, and with a nod of thanks they went back to work.

As soon as the door closed, Shane was on his way to Mariah. Without a word, he pulled her into his arms, then kissed her deeply. "Good morning."

"Good morning to you, too," she said, and wiggled out of his hold, glancing nervously at the door.

"Afraid someone will see us?"

She nodded. "I'd like to keep our private life private."

"Then maybe I can come by your place later?"

"Maybe." She smiled, opened her desk drawer and pulled out the folder he'd given her last night. "You have a few minutes to talk about this proposal before you head out with the crew?"

"You've gone over it already?"

Those big green eyes met his. "I couldn't sleep last night."

His pulse raced. "You, too? You're lucky I wasn't pounding on your door." He pulled up a chair. "What do you think about the Las Vegas project?"

"It's twice the size of Paradise. Can you handle that kind of volume?"

"I've been thinking about expanding the company. I know I could get the crew together. And most of my men wouldn't have a problem doing four to six months in Vegas."

"I agree. This is a good project to bid on," Mariah said. "The time frame and completion dates are reasonable."

Shane felt his excitement build. "How do you feel about living in Las Vegas temporarily?"

"Me? You're offering me a job?"

"Do you have any plans after Paradise?"

Mariah knew Shane was asking her to be more than the project manager. She shook her head.

He grinned. "Then help me work up a bid."

She opened her desk drawer and took out another file. "Like I said, I couldn't sleep last night."

His blue gaze sizzled, then he went over the pages Mariah had worked on most of the night. "Man, I never could have come up with something this detailed."

"It's part of my job description. I still need to check on cost of materials. If you could convince your best men to go with you, even though you have to supply their housing, you'll save money by hiring local workers to complete the crew."

He looked amazed. "You make me feel I could pull this off. How do you feel about going with me to Vegas to talk to a man about a bid?"

Mariah was thrilled at Shane's confidence in her, but she knew she should turn him down. Her father would be furious if he discovered what she was doing. Going away with a Hunter. As far as Kurt Easton was concerned, she was siding with the enemy.

But she couldn't help herself. "I'd love to go."

Friday night, Shane drove them to Tucson to catch the short flight to Las Vegas. They hadn't broadcast the news of their trip to their families, especially not the fact that they were going together.

After landing and retrieving their luggage, they rented a car and headed to an elite hotel on the strip. Shane had reserved a two-bedroom suite. After he tipped the bellboy, he came back into the sitting area to see Mariah's uneasy look. Not what he wanted for their weekend together.

"Unless you're too tired, I thought we could go have some dinner and look around town."

She smiled. "Give me thirty minutes to get ready."

"You look fine to me." Too good. She had on a pair of tan capris and a black cotton sweater. Her beautiful hair was pulled up in a clip.

Mariah glanced around the room. "I just want to call my mom and let her know I've arrived."

"What did you tell your parents?"

"That I'm interviewing for another job," she said. "Which is true."

Shane watched as Mariah went into her room and closed the door. He hoped they weren't going to be apart much this weekend. Away from Haven and family problems, they didn't have to worry about anything but themselves.

But did they have a chance? Would Easton ever accept the fact that his daughter was dating a Hunter?

The bedroom door opened and Mariah reentered the room. She'd let her hair down and put on some lipstick.

She came toward him, slipped her arms around his neck and kissed him. Hard, deep and hungry. By the time she pulled away, his body was aching for more.

"Not that I'm complaining, but what was that for?"

"I just wanted to start off our evening right. And to thank you for wanting me as your project manager."

"I haven't won the bid yet."

She smiled up at him. "You will. Your reputation is growing."

That wasn't all that was growing. "How about we hold off the celebration until tomorrow? Let's go eat."

He took her hand and led her out of the room, before he forgot all about food. And feasted on her.

Mariah hadn't had so much fun in years. She hadn't been to Las Vegas since college. She'd always been too busy to take time off and had always thought gambling was a foolish waste of time and money. But with Shane she was learning things she never had before. Like playing twenty-one.

"Blackjack," Shane announced when she turned over her hand.

"I won!" she cried.

Shane winked at her. "You sure did," he said as the dealer stacked chips in front of her. Thanks to Shane's coaching, her one-hundred-dollar start had grown, and now she'd tripled her stake.

"I think you're buying dinner tomorrow," he told her.

When both of them got bored playing cards, they picked up their chips and wandered toward the slot machines. Shane guided her past the quarter and the dollar machines until they reached the area with the five to twenty-five dollar slots.

"Oh, Shane, I think this is a little too rich for me."

"You've got to live a little." He grinned and pulled out some bills from his pocket. "We'll go in together and see what happens."

Mariah agreed, but after several bills disappeared in

the machine and after several tries, things looked bleak. Then suddenly the three cherries appeared. "Oh, Shane, we won!" she cheered.

"Not enough," he said as he pulled the lever and together they watched the mismatched signs appear in the windows.

After several more times with each taking a turn, nothing happened. Mariah was watching their winnings dwindle. "Maybe we should stop now," she said.

"Where's your adventurous spirit, woman?"

"It flew away with the last hundred dollars."

He leaned forward and placed a lingering kiss on her lips. Then he drew back and winked, causing Mariah to catch her breath. "Trust me," he whispered in a husky voice, then took her hand, raised it to the lever and covered it with his. Never taking his incredible blue eyes off her, he pulled downward.

There was a whirring sound along with the clicks as each window stopped. First a triple bar, then another triple bar and finally the third window joined the other two. Bells went off and Mariah jumped into Shane's arms unaware of the crowd that gathered to see. They'd won almost thirty-five hundred dollars. Shane kissed her. "See, I told you we make a good team."

Around 1:00 a.m., Shane and Mariah reluctantly called it a night. Mariah was hesitant. It had been so long since she let loose and had a good time. Of course spending the evening with Shane Hunter would be any girl's perfect fantasy. And tonight that was what this was. A fantasy. A night off for a little fun.

It all had to end though.

They stepped off the elevator on their floor and headed to the room. But when Shane placed a protective hand against her back and guided her to the door, she couldn't control the shiver. She didn't want him to let her go.

Shane used the key card and opened the door, allowing her to go inside first. The lights had been dimmed and drapes opened to the Vegas glow. She walked to the balcony door, knowing she should say goodnight and go to her room.

"We should call it a night," Shane told her as he came up behind her. "We have to be up early tomorrow."

Mariah wanted to protest, but finally she nodded, expecting him to leave her. Instead, she felt his hands on her shoulders.

"Thanks for tonight, Mariah. I had a lot of fun."

She turned around. "I did, too," she whispered. "Not to mention, it was profitable."

Shane's million dollar grin appeared. "We make a good team."

She let out a long breath. "I hope the same thing happens tomorrow."

He reached out and touched her face. "I'm confident

that there's nothing we can't do…" He lowered his head and placed a soft kiss against her lips. "Together." Finally his mouth covered hers, muffling her gasp. He drew her against him and deepened the kiss. His tongue moved along her lips until she opened and he dipped inside to taste her. Her legs grew weak as her pulse shot up. When he finally released her they were both breathing hard.

"As much as I hate to end this incredible night, I'd better before we get carried away." He kissed the end of her nose, then escorted her to her bedroom door. "Thanks again for tonight, Mariah." He raised her hand to his lips and kissed it. "I'll see you in the morning."

Mariah could only stand there as he walked away, then finally she heard the closing of his bedroom door. She ached to go after him, but knew she couldn't. They couldn't start up something that would be disastrous for everyone concerned.

The fantasy was over.

Their luck had continued the next morning when they went to pitch their bid for the group of custom homes set along a golf course. The investors and architect had more than a passing interest in their ideas, and when Mariah mentioned the well-known projects she'd worked on, they were more than interested and wanted to know when they could start the project.

Back at the hotel, Shane convinced Mariah that they

should go out to celebrate. He sent her down to the hotel boutique to shop for a special dress.

Mariah went shopping but with her own money. And she did find the perfect outfit, a pale-pink dress with thin straps, a narrow waist and a flowing skirt that ended about midcalf in a scalloped hem. She found a pair of pink high-heeled sandals that matched the dress perfectly. She even splurged to have her hair and makeup done.

At six that evening, there was a soft knock on her bedroom door. She drew a breath and opened it, and had difficulty finding her voice as she glanced over the tall man in the dark suit, with a white shirt and burgundy tie. Shane was gorgeous.

"Mariah…you look beautiful," he told her.

"So do you," she breathed.

"I guess I clean up pretty well." He gathered her into his arms, and his mouth came down on hers in an eager kiss. She wrapped her arms around his neck as he teased her lips apart and tasted her. Her body instantly responded to his, just as if she'd been accustomed to his nearness, his touch.

Shane tore his mouth away and pressed his forehead against hers. "I want you, Mariah Easton. I want you like I've never wanted anyone in my life. And if I don't get you out of this room, I'm going to rip off that beautiful dress."

Her pulse raced. "Maybe I want you to do just that," she challenged.

Shane froze, afraid to believe Mariah's words, also knowing they still had so many obstacles to overcome. "You mean that?" He looked down at her. "You want me to make love to you?"

Her gaze met his and nodded.

"What about your father? The feud?"

"It's not our feud." Mariah rose up on her toes and kissed him. "When Catherine married your grandfather it was because they loved each other. That's the only reason two people should be together."

"That's the reason we should be together." He took her mouth in a long searing kiss. "Mariah, marry me?"

Mariah couldn't think rationally. She hadn't since Shane had come back into her life. She found herself nodding in agreement to his wild, unbelievable, wonderful suggestion.

Before she could change her mind, Shane had her in a cab on the way to city hall for a license, then back in the taxi headed to the chapel. His encouraging words had her breathless; his kisses had her dazed. All she wanted was to marry the man she loved. Then everything would be perfect. It had to be.

Shane handed her a bouquet of white roses and stood beside her as the minister began. Her eyes were focused solely on Shane as she heard the words, "I now pronounce you husband and wife."

Then Shane's mouth captured hers. Mariah was lost

totally. He finally broke it off and smiled down at her. "Well, Mrs. Hunter. What do you say we go back to the hotel and celebrate?"

Chapter Eight

It took Shane three tries to get the key card into the slot, but he finally got the hotel door open. He turned to Mariah and swept her up into his arms.

"I want to do this right," he said as he carried his bride over the threshold. Mariah's arms went around his neck and his mouth covered hers. When she whimpered and pressed closer he felt his body respond rapidly.

He pulled back and sucked in a breath. "Maybe we should slow things down a minute." He brought her into the center of the suite where a table, draped in a white linen cloth and lit by tall white tapers, held their wedding supper. Scattered around the room were more flickering candles along with several bouquets of flowers.

"Oh, Shane," Mariah gasped. "How did you arrange all this?"

"With a telephone call." He set her down. "I wanted tonight to be special." He kissed her, then quickly released her. He walked to the table and took the bottle of champagne from the ice bucket and began to open it. "I know we rushed the wedding, but that doesn't mean we can't make this night memorable." The cork popped, and his gaze went to his new wife.

Shane waited for panic to set in, but all he could think was how beautiful she looked and how much he wanted her. He turned away to pour the wine, and discovered his hands were a little shaky. He walked back to Mariah and handed her a glass.

"To my beautiful bride," he toasted, and they both took a drink.

He couldn't stop looking at her. "Tell me I'm not dreaming, Mariah. That I'm going to wake up and you'll be gone."

She took a step closer. "I'm real, Shane. And I'm your wife." She rose up on her toes and kissed him, lingering to nibble on his lower lip, then kissed her way to his ear and whispered, "So, when does the honeymoon start?"

Shane swallowed hard as desire shot through him like a rocket. He groaned and took another drink of champagne. "I thought we could start with dinner." His gaze locked with Mariah's bewitching green eyes. "You're probably hungry—"

Mariah finished her wine and set her glass on the table. "I am hungry." She glanced toward his bedroom. "But not for food."

Somehow Shane managed to swallow the rest of his drink. "Neither am I," he admitted.

He fought to stay calm as his mouth closed over hers, outlining the shape of her perfect lips with his, loving the softness and the texture. She answered by opening to him, letting him slide his tongue against hers. Need surged through him—a kind of need he'd never experienced before. He wanted to absorb all of her.

Mariah couldn't believe Shane was her husband. Suddenly panic hit her, and her mind whirled in confusion with her feelings of love for this man. And worry. She'd wanted this marriage so badly. But did they have a chance? Her father hated Shane. And she loved them both. Why did she have to choose one over the other?

Goose bumps skittered up her spine, and she pushed everything out of her head, everything but now and Shane. Her fingers snaked up his broad chest before coming to rest on his shoulders. She pulled him closer, giving in to her escalating passion.

He cupped her bottom, aligning their bodies from breast to thigh. He tore his mouth away and swept kisses across her cheek, causing her to shiver.

Effortlessly he swung her up into his arms and carried her into his bedroom. There were more candles adorning the nightstands next to the king-size bed. As if waiting for them, the covers were drawn back.

He set her down beside the mattress. "I've dreamed about this since we first met."

"I'm glad that we waited," she admitted shyly. She might be a dozen years older, but she hadn't gained much experience since high school.

He captured her mouth again, then pulled back and smiled as he began to tug the zipper on her dress. "I think you should remove this before I destroy it. And I want tonight to be perfect."

She felt an exhilarating blend of passion and promise. She looked at his face and admitted. "Being with you will be everything I've ever dreamed of."

"I've had more than one fantasy about us myself."

He tugged the dress off her shoulders, and it slid down her body. She stood there in only a sheer bra and panties. His eyes grew heavy-lidded as he stared at her breasts, then he reached out and smoothed one nipple with his thumb. She gasped, aching for more. He rewarded her and leaned down to place his mouth over one tight bud. Her head fell back. Her stomach muscles tightened in anticipation as he laid her down on the cool sheets. He straightened, pulled off his shirt and dropped it on the floor. Next came his boots, his belt, trousers…everything. Her breathing stopped completely as she boldly examined his perfect naked form.

When her gaze returned to his face, she was soon

mesmerized by the intensity in his eyes. He came to her then, and his mouth swooped down on hers, hot and hungry.

He broke off the kiss and gazed down at her body. "You are so beautiful." He released her bra and his callused hands stroked her breasts. Then he sucked and teased her until she whimpered in need and arched toward him. She forgot everything else but this man.

"I want you, Mariah."

"Show me. Make love to me, Shane," she breathed as her hands skimmed over his chest. Their journey continued to his back, and she pulled him against her. "Now."

Shane was beyond resisting her any longer as he stripped off her panties. Bracing his arms on either side of her, he situated himself between her thighs and pushed slowly into her.

He groaned as a sudden tightness knotted his gut and he fought to hold back. It was sweet agony. He'd wanted her for so long...loved her so long. When Mariah wrapped her legs around him and urged him on, he picked up the pace. She quickly learned the rhythm and met him thrust for thrust. He felt her body tighten and she sobbed as she reached for him.

"Shane!" she cried out.

He couldn't hold back any longer and tumbled over the edge with his own climax, collapsing against her. Regaining some strength, he rolled to one side and gathered her into his arms, kissing her hair, lightly stroking her damp skin.

Emotions clogged his throat as he realized he loved her. He'd always loved her. "That was…incredible," he breathed raggedly.

Mariah nodded as she turned to him. There were tears in her eyes. "Oh, Shane…" she whispered.

He hugged her against him. "Don't cry, babe, or at least tell me they're happy tears."

"They're happy. It's just that being with you was so…amazing."

This time he grinned. "Yeah, we were pretty amazing, weren't we?" He pushed her onto her back and kissed her again, deep and long. Then he pulled back only to begin nibbling the underside of her jaw. "Did I ever tell you how crazy I am about you, Mrs. Hunter?"

She felt the urge to giggle, but once again the outside world crept into this private place, causing doubts. "We did act a little crazy. We came here to bid on a job and we got married."

Shane cupped her face, making her look at him, so she couldn't avoid the sincerity in his blue eyes. "And I'm not sorry. Are you?"

A thrill rushed through her as more tears filled her eyes. "Oh, Shane, this is going to cause such a stir. But, no, I'm not sorry."

"Man, I'm sure glad." He placed a hard kiss on her mouth, renewing her desire. He shifted over her, pressing his lower body against hers. She gasped. "Let's just see if we can find paradise again."

At dawn the next morning, Shawn couldn't take his eyes off the sleeping Mariah. She was his wife. He still couldn't believe it. The thought of being responsible for another person was a little scary, especially since he wasn't exactly ready for this. He was still building his business. He'd used most of his profits to pay back the money Nate had loaned him to start Hunter Construction. Now if only the Paradise project was completed on time and he got the promised bonus, he'd be set. But until that happened, he would have to take Mariah to live in his small apartment...just for a while.

Shane's thoughts went to the sweet piece of property he owned just outside of town. About a year ago he'd taken it in on trade for a construction job. The only thing was, he hadn't had the time or money to build on the land. Maybe it was time he did something about that.

He glanced at his bride lying next to him. Mariah's fiery hair flared out against the pillow. He ran his fingers over her soft cheek. She had to be tired, since neither one of them had slept much during the night.

His breath caught as he recalled that she'd been just as hungry for him as he'd been for her. Nothing had changed in all those years apart. His body stirred. He wanted her again.

Unable to resist, Shane leaned down and placed a kiss against her tempting mouth. Before he could pull back, she began to respond and her hands slid to his chest, then around his neck.

He drew back. "Good morning."

She blinked. "Now, remind me again who you are."

He did just that as he flipped her on her back and lay on top of her. His mouth worked its way down her body until she was squirming and begging for more.

"Please, Shane," she said.

"I thought you'd remember me," he teased.

"How could I forget?" she said reaching for him, pulling his mouth back to hers. "Make love to me," she whispered, in between her own form of torture.

"I guess I'll have to work on making it so memorable you won't forget me again." His mouth and hands began to fulfill that promise when the phone rang.

"Ignore it," Shane said. He wasn't about to let anything interrupt his time with Mariah.

Mariah sat up. "We can't."

"Okay, but remember where I was," he said as he reached for the receiver. He was going to get rid of whoever had the nerve to call at this hour. "Hello."

"Hunter," Kurt Easton's angry voice rang in his ear. "I demand to know what the hell you are doing with my daughter."

"I don't have to answer to you for anything except the project," he said. "This is the weekend, Kurt."

"I don't give a damn what day it is. You have a re-sponsibility to your job. That means 24/7. Now, let me talk to Mariah. And don't bother to tell me she isn't with you. I've called her room."

How did Easton know he'd left town? Rod was the only one who knew where to contact him. He prayed there wasn't any trouble.

As he handed Mariah the receiver, Shane watched as the color drained from her face. He wished there was some way he could handle this for her, but he knew she had to be the one to stand up to her father.

She took the phone. "Yes, Dad," she said.

Shane walked across the room and tried not to lis-ten to Mariah's conversation as he slipped on his boxers. Her father had been going through a lot with his recent illness, and Shane also knew that Easton would do anything to keep his daughter away from him.

"Yes, we'll be back later today." She nodded. "I'll come by tonight for dinner. Bye, Dad." With the sheet bunched against her breasts, Mariah reached over and hung up the phone.

"Dad had to go to the E.R. last night. He's okay now, but when I didn't come to see him, Mom told him I flew here for a job interview."

"I guess when we get back we'll have a lot more to tell him."

Mariah's nervous gaze met his. "Shane, we can't tell him we're married. Not now, anyway. He's not well."

This wasn't what Shane wanted to hear. "So, now you're saying this all was…a mistake?"

She climbed out of bed, dragging the sheet with her. "No, I didn't say that. But there's so much at stake right now. We have the project, and Dad just isn't ready to handle this." She placed a hand on his chest. "Please, Shane. Let's just keep this between us for a while. Just until Dad's condition stabilizes."

He didn't have a choice. "Just until he's stable," he repeated, and leaned down to capture her mouth. Even now it didn't take much to stir his desire for her.

Mariah pulled away. "Shane, we need to get an earlier flight. I told Dad I'd be home as soon as possible." She pointed to her bedroom. "I'll call the airline while you shower." She gave him a quick kiss and hurried out of the bedroom.

He could only watch her go. "I guess the honeymoon is over."

That evening Mariah sat at the Eastons' dining room table, pushing her dinner around her plate. The last thing she wanted was food. She wanted to be with her husband.

Shane had dropped her off at her apartment after their trip back from Tucson. They hadn't talked on the plane ride home, either. It disappointed her that he hadn't asked about seeing her later. Of course, she couldn't blame him. They were married, but no one could know that…yet.

"You're not eating your chicken, honey," her mother said. "Are you feeling all right?"

Cheryl Easton always amazed her. The attractive blonde had turned fifty-two last January. She was trim and dressed in designer clothes. Her face was made up perfectly, her nails neatly manicured. She'd provided her husband a perfect home and raised two well-mannered children. Never once had Mariah heard the woman say a cross word to her husband. And she'd never stand up to him.

"I'm fine, Mom."

"You're definitely not fine when you run off and spend the weekend with a Hunter," her father said. "I don't want you seeing Shane again."

Her temper flared. "Dad, I work with him. Besides, I'm old enough to decide who I see."

He glared at her. "So it doesn't matter that I'll be a laughingstock when everyone hears that my daughter ran off to Las Vegas with the likes of Shane Hunter. The man is nothing but a womanizer."

She felt the heat rush to her cheeks. That was true. Shane had dated a lot of women. "How will anyone know, unless you tell them?"

Her brother dropped his fork on the plate. "How can you stand to be around that jerk?" Rich's anger was obvious as he glared at her. "So I guess you've gone over to *their* side."

"Rich, there are no sides." She looked at her father.

"Shane had nothing to do with what happened sixty years ago." She stood. "I need to go."

Thank God no one tried to stop her as she marched out of the house. She'd had enough, but before she made it to her car she heard her mother call to her.

"Mariah, don't leave like this. Your father doesn't need to be upset."

She sighed. "Mom, I'm just so tired of this. I want to help Dad, but the hatred he has for the Hunters isn't good for him, either." Good Lord, what was going to happen when he found out that Shane was his new son-in-law?

"We need to help him, Mariah."

"I don't think I can. I won't let him tell me who I can be with."

"I know. And I know you care about Shane. You've always had feelings for him. Back in high school, I know you used to sneak off to be with him."

"How come you never stopped me?"

"Because I had enough to handle with your father's…problem. I have nothing against Shane. He seems like a nice young man. He was always polite to me, even when he came by and I told him you didn't want to see him."

Mariah's heart pounded in her chest. "When?"

"The day of your going-away party. I just didn't want to upset your father."

"Mom, you should have told me."

"I was going to, but it wasn't the best time for your father, with you going away and all."

Mariah knew what "and all" meant. Her father had still been drinking. It had been the main reason she'd been so eager to leave for college. But Shane had wanted to see her. Had he been trying to stop her? "You still should have told me."

"Maybe the reason I didn't was that I knew you both cared so much for each other. And since you and Shane went away for the weekend together, I guess you still do."

Mariah wanted to confide in her mother about her feelings, her marriage, but that would put her in the middle. Mariah refused to put her mother in a position where she would have to choose between her daughter and her husband. "Yes, I care about Shane..."

With a nod her mother reached for Mariah's hand. "You're too old for me to tell you what to do. And I doubt it would do any good. Just don't flaunt it in your father's face. He's gone through a lot lately with Nate buying back the Double H, and Shane's company winning the bid on the Paradise project. And now with his illness. Just take things slow."

It was a little late for that. "Mom, this is so ridiculous. The Hunters aren't out to get the Easton family. You have Granddad Easton to thank for starting this mess, but I blame Dad for carrying on the feud and passing his prejudice on to Rich."

Like a devoted mother, she defended her son. "Rich is a good boy. He just wants his father's attention and acceptance."

Mariah wasn't so sure. "Mom, why doesn't Rich come to work at the site? He can handle weekends until school is out. He can earn some spending money."

"Do you think that's such a good idea?"

"It's a great idea. He can see for himself that Shane isn't a bad guy. They could get to know each other."

Her mother sighed. "I'll suggest it, if you'll continue to come by to see your father. I know he's made a lot of mistakes over the years, but he loves you."

"I love him, too." She loved them all. Her father, her brother and her husband. They just happened to hate each other.

Later that evening Shane sat on the top step of Mariah's apartment when she finally pulled up. His heart raced when she got out of the car and started to climb the stairs.

She looked good dressed in her jeans and sleeveless gold blouse. Her hair lay in soft curls against her shoulders. He wanted to take her in his arms and kiss her senseless, until she admitted she wanted him more than anything else.

Finally she noticed him. "Shane, what are you doing here?"

"Hi." He stood. "I thought we should talk."

"Funny, you didn't have much to say on our trip back from Vegas."

He shrugged. "I was angry about you wanting to keep our marriage a secret. But I've had some time to think things over."

She climbed the last step to the landing. "And what did you come up with?"

"That I acted like a jerk." He stepped closer. When she didn't back away, he reached out and touched her hair. "And, God, I missed you. I couldn't stop thinking about you—about us. How much I hate fighting with you." He leaned down and nibbled on her mouth. "I'd much rather make love to you."

She sighed. "Oh, Shane."

Mariah wanted to be strong, to resist this man until she had time to figure things out. That was until she saw him on her doorstep, dressed in snug jeans and a western shirt that emphasized his broad shoulders. Then with one come-hither look from him, she turned to mush.

He drew her into his arms and kissed her as if he never meant to stop. Searing heat radiated between them as his hands skimmed over her, slipped inside her jeans pockets and cupped her bottom. She felt as if she would die right on the spot as he molded her to his body.

He broke off the kiss. "Let's take this inside."

She handed him her key. He unlocked the door and pulled her into the apartment. There was a light on beside the bed, washing the small room in a soft, intimate glow.

He turned back to her, taking her face between his hands as he trailed kisses along her cheek, then her closed eyelids. "Being with you last night was incredible. It's only been about twelve hours, but it seems like an eternity." His voice was husky with need, his breathing rapid. So was hers. He ran his hands into her hair and bent his head to kiss her again. "Just tell me you want me, too."

Mariah's desire for this man blocked out all reason, all common sense. "Oh, Shane, yes." She pulled his head down so she could take his mouth, absorb his heat, the taste of him. Her hand moved over his chest, pulling at the shirt. Once the snaps gave way, Shane stripped off the garment and then went to work on her clothes.

A sudden knock on the door caught both their attentions.

"Who is it?" she called.

"Mariah, it's Nate. I'm looking for Shane."

"I'm here, Nate." Shane fumbled to straighten his clothes, trying not to worry why his brother had tracked him down. He slipped on his shirt while Mariah discreetly went into the bathroom.

Shane opened the door. "Nate, what's wrong?"

His brother didn't look happy. "We couldn't reach you, so I came by to get Mariah when I saw your truck."

"Something happen at the site?" Shane asked, already concerned by the look on Nate's face.

He nodded. "Someone was taking target practice at the model home's windows."

"Damn. When is this nightmare going to end?" Shane worked at buttoning his shirt.

"Sorry, by the time your security contacted us, they were gone."

"Are Roger and Jerry okay?"

"They're fine. I told them to stay put until we get there."

"I guess I should be grateful for that." He tucked in his shirt and ignored the questioning look on his brother's face. He slipped on a jacket just as Mariah walked out of the bathroom.

There wasn't time for awkwardness or to exchange greetings. Shane grabbed her hand and they were out the door. Right now he had to stop whoever was trying to ruin him.

Chapter Nine

It only took ten minutes to get to the site in Nate's patrol car. Shane had the door open before the vehicle came to a stop. He hurried across the lot to survey the damage and found the security guard, Roger, talking with Deputy Clark.

"Did you at least get a look at them?" Shane asked, though he already knew he wasn't going to get the answer he wanted.

Roger shook his head. "Sorry, Shane. Jerry and I chased them to the ridge." The guard pointed past the row of structures. "By the time we got up there, they'd spotted us. We heard a truck start up and they hightailed it out of there."

"Damn." Shane was fed up with this. "Why are they

doing this? What is the point? You'd think that they would be more interested in stealing something valuable. All they're doing is causing destruction."

Shane felt Mariah come up beside him. He turned to her. He loved her beauty, her touch, but right now he needed her strength and support.

"Once it's daylight, maybe Nate can come up with some evidence," she said.

Shane nodded. As badly as he wanted answers, he wasn't going to get them tonight. "I guess we should check out the damage." They started toward the trio of two-story Tudor-style homes. He gripped Mariah's hand as they made their way up the hill to one of the nearly completed models. He took a large flashlight from Roger and shone it against the front of the house to the missing leaded and beveled-glass picture window. Damn. He shifted the light around and realized some of the wood framing had been splintered by the shells.

"Aw, hell. This one was going to be our first model home. The interior decorator was coming in this week to get it ready for the open house next month." He raised the light to the second story and found more destruction. "How are we going to replace these windows in time? They were a special order. It took us weeks to get them," he murmured more to himself then anyone else.

Mariah stood close to his side. "I can make some calls."

Frustration made him lash out. "What good will it do? They'll just come back and do something else. Hell, I can't keep replacing everything. It's eating into the profits as it is."

"What about the insurance?"

"The red tape will take more time than we have. You know it's about time as much as the money." He glanced at Nate. "What else can I do? How can I stop these bastards?"

Nate straightened. "Not going off half-cocked would be a good idea. You have to leave this to the law."

"No offence, bro, but you haven't exactly been much help." Shane quickly regretted his words. "I'm sorry."

Nate nodded. "I'm sorry, too. I don't have the manpower to keep a deputy out here round the clock. We have to hope these guys make a mistake."

A set of headlights lit the area as a town car pulled up and Kurt Easton got out.

"Great, he's all I need," Shane growled.

Mariah suddenly dropped her hand from Shane's arm and went to her father. Without as much as a hello, Easton took the flashlight from Shane and turned toward the house. After about thirty seconds he finally spoke. "Sheriff, what are you doing about this?"

"Can't do anything tonight," Nate said. "Tomorrow we'll check Rock Ridge and hope they got careless and left some evidence behind."

Easton looked at Shane. "I blame you for this. You

should be concentrating on this project, not in Las Vegas looking for another job."

Shane couldn't hold back any longer. "You're just loving this, aren't you, Easton? You love it even more that you get to blame me. That this makes me look bad."

Easton shrugged. "It's not my problem that you can't handle the job."

Nate stepped in. "I think you all should just cool off.

Mariah added. "Dad, Shane had nothing to do with this trouble."

"He didn't prevent it, either."

"Like I haven't tried," Shane said, fighting to control his anger. "I've hired more security, added floodlights. It's as if they have inside information. They seem to know the schedules of the personnel." They always seem a step a head of me, he added silently. "It's getting too personal. As if someone wants me to fail."

"You're doing that all by yourself," Kurt sneered.

"Hell, Easton, I wouldn't be surprised if you weren't behind this somehow."

Mariah gasped. "Shane. Dad wouldn't do that. He has as much to lose as you do."

Shane looked from Easton to Mariah. His heart slipped into his gut as his wife sided with her father against him. "Not as much as I do," he said, and he wasn't thinking about the Paradise project.

Mariah saw the pain in Shane's eyes and knew she'd

caused it. How could she choose between the two men she loved? "I think in the morning we'll all have clearer heads and be able to talk this out."

"I've said all I have to say." Shane turned and marched off toward the trailer.

Mariah shot a sharp look at her father. "You know, if you are so worried about the project, I think you would find a way to help out. When I agreed to take this job, I told you I didn't want this to happen."

"That was before you went off on your tryst with Hunter."

Mariah bit down on her anger as she thought about her father's recent illness. "I'm old enough and have been on my own far too long to have to explain my personal life." She hurried to catch up with Shane. "Shane, wait, I want to talk to you."

He kept walking. "Why? You made your position clear," he tossed over his shoulder.

She reached for him and made him stop. "What did you expect? You accused my father of sabotaging this job."

"It makes sense to me. Who else has it in for me? Who else would love to see a Hunter fall on his face? Well, honey, I'm stumbling pretty good right now."

She glanced toward the damaged houses. He was making her doubt her father's innocence. "Dad would never go this far." She prayed that she was right.

"When it comes to the Hunters, he goes as far as he can."

"Shane, I know for a fact that he has nearly everything tied up in this project."

"So do I. This is my beginning, Mariah. This is our future. Or, at least, I thought we had a future together." The blue-eyed gaze she loved so much suddenly turned cold. "Now I'm not so sure."

Mariah was hurt by his lack of faith in her. She should be used to it, Shane had hurt her before. He had turned on her before. You would think she'd have learned her lesson by now. How could she think there could ever be a future for them? "Neither am I."

Suddenly she heard her name called and glanced back at her father who was leaning against the car. He looked exhausted. "I need to get Dad home." She paused hoping Shane would say he was sorry, and take her in his arms.

"We were wrong, Mariah. Our getting married will never stop the feud. Kurt Easton is never going to accept me." Shane turned away when her father called her again. "You'd better get going."

Her heart lurched painfully. Well, she didn't need to be told twice. "Goodbye, Shane." Fighting tears, she walked away. What was she going to do now? How was she supposed to recover from a second broken heart?

Shane arrived at the site early the next morning to meet Nate at Rock Ridge. They scoured every inch of ground and found several empty casings from a rifle.

Nate bagged the evidence for fingerprints. But unless the vandals had criminal records it was a waste of time.

"I know it's not much to go on, but we could get lucky," Nate said.

"I'm not going to rely on luck anymore. I'm moving into the trailer until this job is finished. And I'm not going to let anyone take what's mine." He continued, again thinking more about Mariah than the project.

"You still believe Kurt had something to do with this?"

"I doubt he'd get his hands dirty, but I wouldn't put it past him to hire someone." Shane sighed. "If it were teenagers, wouldn't they have given up by now?"

His brother looked at him. "Just be careful, Shane. If these guys are pros, they might play rough."

"I've got to put a stop to this."

"Like I said, be careful." Nate paused a moment. "Tell me to mind my own business, but I take it that things are serious between you and Mariah."

Serious enough that he'd married her. "Twenty-four hours ago I might have thought so."

His brother clapped him on the shoulder. "If you want to talk, I'm here." They started back for the trailer.

"Thanks, but I don't think talking is going to help," Shane said.

"To quote my beautiful wife, 'Spoken like a typical stubborn male.'" Nate smiled as he climbed into the patrol car and headed off toward town.

Shane glanced toward the damaged house. The crew was already beginning the clean up. This wasn't what he wanted his men to be doing this morning. He turned toward the space where Mariah usually parked her truck. It was empty.

After the things he'd said to her, he couldn't blame her for not showing up today. But all he wanted was for his wife to stand by him. Was that too much to ask? Perhaps it was, when he acted like a jackass.

He walked inside and on his desk he discovered a manila envelope. It was from Mariah. He opened the folder and a note dropped out. He began to read,

Shane,
I contacted the Exclusive Window Company and ordered the replacements for the two model homes. They've guaranteed delivery and installation in three weeks for our deadline. I've used them before, and their product is excellent. And they've always come through. If you have a problem with me overstepping my authority, there's a twenty-four-hour cancellation period.

I won't be coming to the site for a while, but don't worry, I'll get my work done. I feel we both need time to think things through and decide what path to take. Please don't try and contact me right now.
Mariah

Shane couldn't find enough air in his lungs as he sank into the chair. How did things get so messed up? He rubbed his hands over his face. All he wanted was what he's always wanted, Mariah. And for a while she'd been within reach.

It tore him up inside to remember their time together in Las Vegas. He'd had it all. Mariah had become his wife, and their lovemaking had been incredible. Those forty-eight hours had been the closest thing to heaven he'd ever known.

He thought back to last night and how torn Mariah had looked. He never wanted her to regret marrying him. If that meant he had to back off, give her the time, he'd do it.

Besides, he knew he had to clear things up here first. He had to show Kurt Easton that he could handle this project before he could start his life with Mariah. A smile touched his lips. Just wait until that man learned that a Hunter was his son-in-law.

A week later Mariah's mother decided they needed to get out of the house. Cheryl Easton thought the cure for everything was walking through the crowded Tucson Mall, trying on clothes and shoes. Mariah hated shopping, and her wardrobe showed it. But now she had several new outfits that she'd probably never get the chance to wear. When would she have the opportunity? Her thoughts turned to the lavender sundress she'd found in a little boutique. The thin straps and fitted bodice showed off her waist. She couldn't help but wonder if Shane would like it. Would he think she looked sexy? The memory of how quickly he'd stripped off her pink dress on their wedding night was still vivid in her mind.

Warmth spread through her as she shook away the sensual image. She released a long breath, knowing she had too much time on her hands. She needed to get back to work.

Thanks to her laptop computer, and to Rod for letting her know when Shane left the site, she'd been able to get to her desk and keep up with her duties. The last thing she wanted was to run into Shane. Yet a part of her hoped that she would. She was starved for him, his touch, his kisses. And even though she'd asked him not to contact her, she'd prayed he would. But he hadn't called or stopped by.

Tears sprang to Mariah's eyes as the familiar pain tightened her chest. Shane had made it perfectly clear that she wasn't worth fighting for. Everything was such a mess. Why did she have to fall in love with Shane? Why did she have to go with him to Las Vegas? Why had she let him make incredible love to her? Had it meant anything to him at all? A tear found its way down her cheek. Did she mean anything to him?

"Wasn't this morning fun?" Her mother's voice broke into her reverie.

Mariah quickly wiped away the tears. "It was nice,

Mom." Before heading home after shopping they stopped for lunch at the café and made their way to an empty booth.

"It's been forever since we've had a day together just to shop." Cheryl Easton took her daughter's hand. "I just wish I could get your mind off your troubles."

"I doubt you can get Dad to lay off Shane."

Her mother sighed. "Oh, honey, I've tried for years. I know this silly feud has taken a toll on him, especially on his health." Her mother raised an eyebrow. "And now it's affecting you. Again."

Mariah opened her mouth, but no denial came. "I care about Shane." She shook her head. "I didn't plan on that."

"And you still love him," her mother added.

"Yes, but it doesn't help matters. Dad and Shane hate each other. How can I choose between them?"

"You may have to, Mariah. Years ago I knew how much you cared for Shane, but you both were so young then. And when he broke your heart it was hard for me to see your sadness." Her mother sighed. "So I was happy when you decided to go away to school. I was hoping you'd forget about Shane and find someone else. But it seems you didn't."

It was useless to deny the obvious. Mariah shook her head as a tear found her cheek. "Oh, Mom, what am I going to do? I was crazy to think I could come back here and work with Shane as if the past hadn't happened. It hurts so much."

The older woman reached across the table for her daughter's hand. "Oh, honey, I wish I had some answers for you. Believe me, after living with your father all these years, all I can say is you have to take the good with the bad. And you just have to love men even when they're stubborn and stupid."

"That's just it. I love Shane. And I'm miserable."

Her mother glanced toward the door. "And I'd bet Shane isn't feeling much better. Don't worry, honey. If it's meant to be, everything will work out in the end."

Mariah sighed. She hoped her mom was right, but didn't see any simple way out of this situation.

Shane walked into the café and sat down at the counter. He wasn't a bit hungry, but his mother had threatened him with bodily harm if he didn't show up and eat something.

At least the lunch crowd had tapered off. He wasn't in the mood to be sociable. What he wanted was to go home and sleep like the dead for the next two days. But it didn't look like that was going to happen until the project was completed, or the vandals were caught. Maybe then things would get back to normal.

Yeah, sure. He knew his life would never be normal again. Feeling anxious, he twisted around on his stool toward the door, when a flash of auburn hair caught his attention.

His gaze stopped at the booth by the window where Mrs. Easton and Mariah sat. His hungry gaze searched his bride's face. Her pale, flawless skin, her glorious hair. He recalled those wild curls spread out on the pillow as he made love to her. His breathing stopped as his attention went to her mouth, and her relived how her lips felt against his heated skin.

As if she sensed him watching her, she raised her emerald gaze to his. His stomach tightened. God, he missed her. The ache spread into his chest as Gene Pitney's, "Half Heaven, Half Heartache," began to play on the jukebox.

His mother appeared. "Shane, you made it."

He blinked and stood to offer his mother the seat next to his. "You didn't give me a choice," he said as the waitress dropped off two glasses of water. He took a long drink, hoping it would cool him off.

"Someone has to look out for you."

Betty Hunter was an attractive woman and she took care of her health. Although a strong person, she'd had to handle a lot in her life. After the death of her husband when she was in her forties, she'd lost her home. She had to return to teaching to support her family; that meant dealing with two rowdy sons and a preteen daughter. Not only did Shane love his mother, he respected and admired her.

"It's nice to know that no matter how many times I screw up you still love me."

His mother cocked an eyebrow. "If I'd known this was a pity party, I would have brought my violin."

"Give a guy a break, I've had a bad week."

She took a drink from her glass. "I've had a few myself. Shall we compare?"

He fought a smile and lost. "I think you'd win."

"That's right. I've also had a lot of good things in my life. You kids for one. You've come a long way, son. Your father would be proud. So don't you let it be overshadowed by one person."

They didn't have to mention Kurt Easton by name. "But that person can break me."

"Then don't let him, Shane. You're doing an excellent job, and the other investors know that."

The waitress appeared and took their food order. After she left, Shane continued. "But I'm losing money and time on this project. I can't afford to hire any more security."

"So you've been at the site every night. You can't run on no sleep, Shane." Betty shook her head. "How does Mariah feel about you staying out there?"

Shane looked away. His mom was too good at reading him. "Mariah's staying close to her dad these days."

Betty sighed. "It's so like Kurt to use his illness to keep her away from you. Maybe there's something I can do to help."

"Mom, Mariah and I aren't exactly seeing each other right now."

"So you did let Kurt get between you."

"I didn't exactly have much to say about it."

His mother didn't look convinced. "Since when haven't you gone after something you wanted? You're as stubborn as your father was. Anything you want badly enough is worth fighting for. How badly do you want Mariah?"

So badly he hurt. "I don't think a Hunter and an Easton are meant to be together."

Just then Sam came out of the kitchen. "Hi, Shane." The older man's gaze gentled as he looked at his mother. "Hi, Betty. How's it going?"

"My son's being stubborn," she said. "Sometimes men can't see what's right in front of them." Then finally his mother said, "I need to go. Cancel my order, Sam. I'll see you later, son." She kissed him and headed for the door.

Shane frowned. Sam and his mother had been close for years. Lately Shane had even thought they were more than friends, which was fine with him. "What just happened here?"

Sam watched as Betty Hunter walked past the picture window. "Let's just say that figuring out what a woman is up to is one of the mysteries of life." He finally turned to look at Shane and smiled. "It's also one of the wonderful things that makes them so darn interesting."

In the mirror over the counter, Shane watched as Mariah and her mother got up from the booth. His heart raced when his wife paused at the door and glanced back at him. Damn. He fought to keep from going to her, taking her in his arms, promising her everything would work out for them. But he couldn't, not yet. Somehow he had to straighten out the mess at the site before he could offer her a future.

Chapter Ten

Another week passed, and Mariah's misery had only gotten worse. The nights had been especially hard as sleep eluded her. How was she expected to sleep when her thoughts were consumed with Shane and memories of their one night of passion in Las Vegas. And when she finally closed her eyes and slept, she'd dream about him. It was all she had.

Wanting privacy and time alone, she moved back into the tiny apartment over the café. It had worked. Her father couldn't bug her, but there was no Shane, either.

She'd never been so lonely in her life.

Mariah's misery was interrupted by a knock on the door. She got up from the bed and took a quick glance in the mirror. She groaned. She was a mess, and definitely not in the mood for company or one of her mother's pep talks. Running her fingers through her hair, she walked barefoot to the door.

Mariah opened the door and was surprised to find Tori Hunter standing on the porch. The petite blonde looked cute in her pink T-shirt and jean overalls that showed off her slightly rounded stomach. Her hair was pulled back into a ponytail.

"Tori."

"Hi, Mariah. Don't you just hate people who stop by uninvited?"

"I was expecting my mother with another casserole."

Tori smiled shyly and held out a pastry box. "I'm bringing you to-die-for chocolate doughnuts."

Mariah's mouth watered, and at the same time a twinge of nausea gripped her stomach. "Please, come in." She stood aside. "Just ignore the mess, I've been trying to get some work done."

"Boy, does this place bring back memories." Tori's gaze filled with emotion as she glanced around the small room. "Did you know that when I first came to town, Nate talked Sam into letting me stay here and giving me a job?"

Mariah gathered up some papers from the unmade bed. She shook her head. "Sam's one of the nice guys." She smoothed out the comforter over the mussed sheets. "Here, sit down. I don't have much to offer you." She glanced down at Tori's stomach. "And you can't have coffee, can you?"

"I have to confess, the doughnuts are just an excuse to come by and see you."

"You don't need an excuse, Tori."

Tori raised an eyebrow. "You may change your mind after you hear what I have to say." She took a breath. "I don't normally interfere, but I can't stand by and see two people who are meant to be together be apart. I love Shane like a brother and he's miserable. And I think you're the cause."

Mariah's chest tightened. "I never meant to—"

"I know," Tori said, looking sad and frustrated. "Nate said I should stay out of whatever is going on between you two."

Mariah's emotions were too fragile for this conversation. "Please, I don't want to talk about Shane."

"I understand, but I just need to say something. I know how it is to be torn. For most of my life, I let my father dictate to me and to manipulate me into doing what he wanted. I wanted his love so badly that I ended up doing everything to please him." She blinked back tears. "In the end it nearly cost me Nate."

Seeing Tori's obvious pain, Mariah's heart went out to her.

"Sorry, I guess it still hurts. But the thing is, Mariah, I don't need to beg for my father's acceptance or love anymore. I have Nate now and soon our baby."

Mariah felt a surge of envy for Tori.

"I'll bet anything that Shane loves you, Mariah. And I think you love him. I know this feud is driving a wedge between you, and I know firsthand how it has affected the Hunter family. And now it's keeping you and Shane from being together."

"It's so much more than the feud," Mariah explained. "We have a history. We couldn't make it work between us way back when, and not much has changed."

"That's because you're letting your father interfere."

That was true. She'd been put in the middle, years ago. And the same thing was happening again. "We both said things, hurtful things… Worse, Shane thinks we made a mistake."

"Made a mistake?" Tori asked.

This time Mariah couldn't stop the tears as they streamed down her cheeks. "We were married in Las Vegas."

Tori's eyes rounded. "Oh, my." Then a big smile spread across her face. "You and Shane were married two weeks ago and you haven't told anyone?"

Mariah swiped at her eyes. "Two weeks and five days," she corrected. "But we've been apart most of that time. I can't blame Shane. I asked him to keep it a secret until my father's health stabilized. Then the night the site was vandalized my father said some things and Shane fired back. I tried to stop the fight, but I just made things worse."

"So Shane's been living out at the site and you've been here, miserable. The story sounds all too familiar. The day Nate got the winning bid on the Double H, we had a horrible misunderstanding. I went back to San Francisco because I didn't think Nate loved me."

"What happened?"

Tori sighed. "I let my father break us up. It was a big mistake. Thank goodness I came to my senses, but before I could get back to Haven, Nate came after me."

Mariah had been hoping Shane would come by the apartment, the way he had that first night. "I don't think Shane is going to come after me, Tori. Not when my father is threatening to fire him."

"I doubt Shane is worried about Kurt Easton. The two things Hunter men care about most are protecting their heritage and the people they love. Nate felt he couldn't ask me to be his wife if he didn't have anything to offer me. Shane's running scared with the trouble at Paradise Estates. He's worked hard to make a go of his company."

"And he has. My father is wrong about him. Shane doesn't have to prove anything to me."

Mariah's head hurt, and she felt sick to her stomach. "I should have stood by him. Now he thinks I'm against him. All I wanted to do was keep the peace."

"Then why don't you tell him that?"

"Now?"

"It's only going to get worse if you wait. I guarantee that Shane isn't going to turn you away. Go to him."

Excitement rushed through Mariah. She stood, but when a sudden dizziness hit her, she groaned and sank back onto the bed.

Tori hurried to her aid. "Here, just lie down." She pressed Mariah's head to the pillow. "Be right back." She left but quickly returned and placed a damp cloth on Mariah's forehead. After a while Tori said. "The dizziness should pass soon."

Mariah groaned. "I just want to die." Nausea threatened her, but finally it subsided, too.

She opened her eyes to see Tori's smiling face. "If my suspicions are correct, I'd say this will be happening for a while. I take it that Shane doesn't know you're pregnant?"

"You got married?" Nate shot Shane an incredulous look from across the trailer. "In Vegas!"

Shane stopped his pacing. "You didn't hear me the first time? Yes! Mariah and I got married." It felt good to say it. That didn't mean anything was going to change. Mariah was at her parents' and he was basically living at the site.

"Then what the hell are you doing here when your bride is somewhere else?"

It was after 4:00 a.m., and Shane had been like a caged animal for days. He'd survived on little or no sleep. The only thing he allowed himself to think about was getting his hands on the person who was out to ruin him. When Nate came by to help out, Shane suddenly started pouring out his troubles to his brother.

"Because Mariah wants it that way."

Nate frowned. "Is that what she told you?"

"Well, not in so many words."

Nate shook his head. "If I've learned anything in the eight months I've been with Tori it's that women don't always say what they mean. They usually want you to come after them."

"Like I'm going to charge over to the Eastons' house. Kurt would love to throw me out on my butt. Thanks, but no thanks. Speaking of wives, how come you left Tori alone in her condition?"

"I didn't. She isn't at the ranch, she's staying with Mom tonight so I can help you out. But this is a bigger job than I expected. Look, bro, you have to go talk to Mariah. The longer you wait, the harder it's going to be to patch things up."

There hadn't been a night since their return to Haven that he hadn't wanted to be with her. Two weeks ago he'd thought his dreams had come true, but then everything got messed up, and hurtful things had been said. "It all happened so fast."

Nate raised an eyebrow. "Are you saying that you don't love Mariah?"

Shane had no problem answering. "I love her. I didn't know how much until—" The image of their night together making love was burned into his head…

just like Mariah was burned into his heart. "Until she walked away. I needed her to stand by me."

"You didn't exactly call her back," Nate said.

"Like you're such an expert. If I remember correctly, there was a time you sent Tori packing off to San Francisco."

Nate cringed. "And I'm trying to keep you from making the same stupid mistake."

Shane ran his fingers through his hair. "Mistakes seem to be my stock in trade. I can't keep Easton off my back. And he's turning Mariah against me."

"Mariah's not against you. But she loves her father. Tori went through the same thing. Even after the great J. C. Sheridan used his daughter as a pawn, she still wanted his love." Nate's eyes grew intense. "And her father's approval was the one thing I couldn't give her." He looked at Shane. "Mariah may have to choose, too. None of us asked for this vendetta Easton has against our family. But Mariah is a Hunter now."

"But for how long?"

Nate smiled. "I've seen how she looks at you. I don't think her feelings have changed since high school. Just keep assuring her that you love her."

Shane glanced away.

Nate groaned. "Tell me you've told her how you feel."

Shane opened his mouth to explain when the radio squawked.

"Shane, it's Jerry. Do you copy?"

Shane picked up the receiver. "Yes, Jerry, I copy. What's going on?"

"There's some activity around the third section. Roger went for a closer look."

Shane glanced at Nate. "Hold your position, Jerry. Nate and I will be there. Over." He headed to the door with Nate on his heels. "I'm going to get him this time," Shane said, feeling his anger building.

"You will. And I'm going to make sure that we do this by the book. I don't want you charged with beating up a suspect, so promise me you won't go off half-cocked. We go by the book or you don't go at all."

Shane wanted nothing more than to take his frustration and anger out on this guy, but he knew he had to keep a cool head. He nodded. "By the book."

Shane and Nate hurried across the compound, making sure they stayed in the shadows so as not to spook the intruder. Finally they reached the tree and Jerry.

"As far as Roger can tell there's only one of them." The security guard pointed toward the frame structure. "He's inside spraying graffiti on the sheet rock."

It was Nate who whispered instructions, "Tell Roger to stay put until we circle around the back."

While Jerry was relaying the message, Nate took Shane's arm. "I'm still the sheriff here so let me be the first to confront this guy. He could be armed."

"Fine. Just so he doesn't get away again." Shane felt

his heart drumming in his chest. "And I want a piece of him," he murmured to himself.

"Okay let's go," Nate said, and they moved silently around the perimeter of the yard where they found Roger hiding toward the back of the structure. Nate drew his weapon and signaled for them to move in.

As they silently approached, only the stinging odor of aerosol paint filled the air. Then a tall, slender silhouette came into view, dressed completely in black, a ski mask covering his face. Shane's heart stopped, then began drumming in his chest.

"This is Sheriff Hunter," Nate called as he took a step closer. "Drop the can and raise your hands."

The intruder froze momentarily, then shot out of the structure and ran toward the foothills.

"Dammit, he's not getting away this time," Shane growled as took off after him. The guy was fast and in good shape, but Shane knew his way around the area and was driven by anger and adrenaline…and the fact he couldn't make a go of his construction business if this guy kept destroying property and supplies. He had to be stopped. So the chase was on, both men tearing through the grove of trees until they reached the moon-lit clearing. Shane was spurred on by his determination and the advantage of now being able to see his prey. And he was going to get him. He had to. He had to be able to fix things with Mariah. He wanted her above anything else.

Shane suddenly put on a burst of speed. He lunged for the intruder, grabbed hold of him and tackled him to the ground. The man fought like crazy, kicking and punching, but Shane outweighed him by a good twenty pounds. He managed to pin his opponent until Nate and the security guard caught up.

While Shane held the other man facedown, Nate drew the vandal's hands behind his back and handcuffed him. "You have the right to remain silent, the right…" Nate began to recite as he pulled him to his feet.

Shane couldn't wait any longer to identify the man who'd caused so much damage. He grabbed the ski mask and yanked it off, only to find himself face-to-face with Rich Easton.

"Well, I'll be damned…" Shane breathed.

The kid fought to break free. "You can't do this. Wait until my dad finds out." He glanced at Nate. "He'll have your badge."

Nate shrugged. "He can have it. I'm a few months from retirement. Right now I'm concerned about you. Do you have any idea how much trouble you're in, son?"

The kid's attitude grew more defiant. "I'm not worried, my dad will get me out of it."

It was only a little after 6:00 a.m. when Mariah pulled her truck into the parking space at the site. She still wasn't sure she was ready to face Shane, especially with her news. Yesterday morning, with Tori's encouragement, she'd taken an early pregnancy test.

The result was positive.

After the first shock eased, she realized she was happy about the idea of having Shane's baby. No matter what the outcome. Even though she wanted the outcome to be a happy life with Shane, but what if he decided he didn't want to continue the marriage…

Mariah shook away the thought. Shane had been the one to call and ask to see her. That was a good sign, wasn't it?

That was when she saw Nate's patrol car parked on the other side of the trailer. What was he doing here so early? As she started up the steps, she saw her dad's car coming down the road.

"Oh, no, not this morning," she murmured. She didn't need another confrontation with him. "Dad, what are you doing here?"

"That's what I'm damn well going to find out," he said as he headed for the trailer. "Then I'm going to meet with the other Paradise investors later and get rid of Hunter."

Mariah sighed. "Why don't you wait until you hear what Shane has to say before you make any decisions?"

Kurt Easton glared at her. "And you've got to get over your infatuation with the guy. He has no future."

"And my personal life is my business." She released

a long breath and pulled open the door. Shane stood at his desk. He looked tired. His clothes were wrinkled, and he had two-days' worth of stubble along his jaw. He had never looked so good to her.

"Mariah." He breathed her name, and she wanted to run into his arms.

"Shane. What's the problem?" She glanced at the other end of the trailer and saw her brother sitting next to Nate.

Her father stepped forward. "Hunter, you better have a good reason to bring me out here at this hour."

Nate stood and took a step forward. "I asked Shane to call you."

That was when Easton noticed the other person on the chair. "Rich?" Kurt said, and he went to his son. It didn't take him long to see the handcuffs. "What's the meaning of this?" He glared at Nate. "Sheriff, you better start giving me some answers."

"It seems that your son, Richard, has been the one vandalizing the site," Nate said.

Easton's face grew red with anger. "That's impossible. There has to be another explanation."

"We caught him right here on the property around 4:00 a.m. this morning. He was armed with a spray paint can in his hands and had painted graffiti on several panels of sheet rock."

Easton's anger seemed to die as he grew pale.

"Shane and I weren't the only ones present," Nate

continued. "The two security guards, Jerry and Roger, were also here when we captured Rich. Roger even identified the ski mask as the same one he's seen before. They signed written accounts of tonight's events."

Mariah trembled as this nightmare unfolded. She watched helplessly as her father went to the sullen boy. "Why, son?" he asked. "Why did you do this?"

Rich blinked, giving him an incredulous look. "Dad, we have to get back at the Hunters for what they did to us." The teenager looked eagerly at his father. Mariah knew how badly her brother wanted Kurt Easton's approval. "Isn't that what you wanted?" Rich asked. "Well, I got 'em good, didn't I?"

Mariah suddenly felt sick. She sank weakly into the chair by the desk. Shane went to her side. "Are you okay?"

She couldn't look at him. She didn't want to see the disgust in his eyes. Yet another Easton had tried to destroy him.

"I don't think I ever will be again," she said as tears flooded her eyes. "I'm so sorry, Shane."

Sobbing, she ran outside, hoping the cool morning air would help her sudden nausea. She gripped her stomach, glad she hadn't eaten anything. She wasn't sure whether the sick feeling was caused by the pregnancy or the shock from her brother's criminal actions.

Shane hurried after her. "Mariah, don't. Don't blame yourself. You had nothing to do with this."

She shook her head. "Does it matter? My father's hatred has gone past being a personal vendetta. My little brother has been infected with it." She stole a look at Shane. "Did you see the look in his eyes? He thought what he was doing was right." Tears rolled down her cheeks. "Why didn't I see how this would turn out?"

"Because you thought he was like every teenager, with a smart mouth and always mad at the world." He moved closer and she could feel his warmth. She wanted his arms around her so badly she trembled with need.

"Rich has to take responsibility for his actions," Shane continued. "You can't do that for him."

"Someone has to be there for him. He's just a kid, Shane. I can't walk away…again. Not this time. Years ago I left him to deal with my father's drinking and, yes, the Easton's vengeance. Maybe if I'd stayed, he would know more than my father's hatred."

Just then the trailer door opened and Nate led her handcuffed brother out the door. Her dad was close behind. He looked in her direction. "Mariah, your family needs you."

She nodded. "I've got to go," she said, though her heart wasn't in it. "For Rich…"

Shane tensed and gripped her arms, stopping her from leaving. "Mariah, you're my wife now," he whispered. "I want to be there for you."

More tears flooded her eyes. She was so ashamed of what her father and brother had done to the Hunter family. "You can't." She took a breath. "I know what

Rich did was wrong, but I'm his sister. He needs my support."

Shane just stood there, and she prayed he wouldn't push the issue, because she was too fragile not to give in to his offer of help.

"I know I've asked you for time, now I have to ask you for patience…just for a while longer."

"Damn. I'd give anything if Rich wasn't involved in this. Believe me, it would make our lives simpler."

Shane pulled her closer, his head only inches from hers. "Just know, Mariah, none of this changes how I feel about you." Then to emphasize his words, he captured her mouth, trying to relay his need, wanting her to forget everything else but what they had together. But, once again, obligations tore them apart.

"Please, Shane, I've got to go."

She was breaking his heart as she stepped back from his embrace and her hand slipped from his. The sudden emptiness was nearly unbearable. He was losing her. "I'm not giving up on us, Mariah. I love you."

She looked stunned at his words, but when her father called she turned away and fled. "Mariah," he called after her. "You're mine. We belong together."

And he meant what he said. He was going to fix it so she didn't leave him again. Even if that meant he had to make a deal with the devil himself.

And that was exactly what he was going to do. He would put an end to this feud once and for all.

Chapter Eleven

At 8:00 a.m. Shane walked into the sheriff's office off Main Street. With a nod to the dispatcher, he continued to Nate's office and shut the door behind him.

His brother looked up from behind his gray metal desk. "You didn't have to come in so early," he said. "A few hours of sleep is justified."

Shane had showered and shaved an hour ago. He had far too much to do today to waste time sleeping.

Nate looked just as tired as Shane felt. "Look who's talking. I bet you haven't been to bed, either."

"I had to process the prisoner."

Shane took a seat in the only other chair in the small office. "Is Rich Easton still in jail?"

Nate brought two mugs filled with hot coffee to the

desk. "No, Kurt got a judge out of bed early this morning. Rich was released into his father's custody. That doesn't mean he doesn't have a lot to answer for."

Shane was just glad it was over. Or was it? Rich was Mariah's brother. "I'm going to ease the burden a little. I'm not going to press charges."

Nate glared at him. "Some of it is out of your hands. Like his shooting off a firearm within city limits."

"But since it's a first offense, I'm sure the judge will go easy on him."

"Is that a good idea? I mean I know you're married to Mariah, but letting the kid get off…"

"Oh, I'm not letting him off. He's going to have to pay for the damages. And not with his father's money, but what he earns by working at the site all summer." Shane smiled. "I'm going to sweat the punishment out of him."

"Think that will make you his favorite brother-in-law?"

"Maybe not, but the kid needs a break."

Before Nate could respond there was a knock on the door and Tori peeked in. "Hey, has anyone seen my husband? A tall, good-looking guy who's about to retire."

Grinning, Nate went to his wife and took her in his arms. "Sorry, haven't seen him. Will I do?" He kissed her thoroughly.

"Maybe," Tori teased.

Shane felt a rush of envy. He wanted the same easy,

loving relationship with Mariah. Doubt hit him, but he pushed it aside. He wasn't going to lose her. He stood. "I better go."

"But you're really the one I came to see," Tori said.

At one time Shane had been attracted to his sister-in-law. But Nate had staked his claim to her, and Shane had backed off. Now Shane loved Tori as a sister and wished his big brother well with her. Although, he never missed an opportunity to rib Nate. Shane hugged Tori to his side. "See, Nate, I told you she liked me the best."

"Go get your own woman."

Tori pulled away. "That's what I came to tell you, Shane," she began. "Mariah loves you very much."

Shane's heart swelled in his chest. "She told you that?"

Tori nodded. "I talked with her yesterday morning. This mess with her brother has got to be rough for her. She really needs you, Shane."

"I'm working on it. I just need…"

The door opened again and Betty Hunter walked in. "Oh, good, Shane, you're here. I went out to the site, but Rod said you'd left."

Shane was a little concerned. "What's the matter, Mom?"

Her concern was evident in her eyes. "Nate called and told me that Rich Easton was involved with the vandalism. Poor Mariah. Have you talked to her?"

Shane shook his head. How could he, when she'd been whisked away by her family? "No, but she's blaming herself for Rich. She thinks if she'd been there for him all along he wouldn't be in this trouble now."

"That's nonsense. If anyone is to blame it's Kurt. He's set a bad example for his son. That boy needs a different male influence."

Nate stepped in. "Shane is going to have plenty of influence with the kid. He plans to give him a job."

Betty's eyes lit up. "Oh, son, that's wonderful."

"Whoa, don't get all excited, I need to talk to Kurt about this." And that wasn't all he needed to discuss with Easton.

"It'll work." His mom sent Shane a bright smile. "And that gives you and Mariah a chance to work things out. Of course, all marriages sometimes have problems and learning how to…"

He glared at his brother. "How did you know Mariah and I were married?"

Nate held up his hands. "I didn't say a word."

Tori gasped. "Nate, when did you find out?"

"Last night, right before we caught our suspect."

Tori turned to Shane. "Mariah told me yesterday morning. I only told Mom because I needed some advice."

Shane sank down on the edge of the desk. "Since everyone knows, would someone help me out here and tell me what I should do?"

His mother came to him. "Go to Mariah and tell her what's in your heart."

He wanted to tell Mariah a lot of things. But the same problem always seemed to come between them. Kurt Easton. It was time to take care of that.

With renewed courage, he started for the door.

"Are you going to see Mariah?" his mother asked.

"First, I need to see a man about a feud."

Shane drove his truck up the private road toward the sprawling two-story house on the hill. He'd only been here once before. Years ago. He'd been frightened then, and he wasn't exactly calm now, but he had too much at stake to turn back now.

Once again Kurt Easton was holding his future in his hands.

Shane came through the open wrought-iron gate, pulled around the circular drive and parked his truck. Before he lost his nerve, he got out, marched up the flagstone walkway to the porch and rang the bell. A surprised Cheryl Easton answered.

"Hello, Mrs. Easton," he said. "I would like to speak to Mr. Easton."

She didn't look pleased at the request. "I'm not sure that is such a good idea, Shane. Everyone is so stressed over this ordeal."

"I'm not planning to add to it, but your husband and I need to get a few things straight."

She finally stepped aside and led him through the large marble-tiled entry, past a winding staircase with a carved-oak railing. He stared in amazement at the impressive artwork grouped along the walls. So Easton had taste.

Mrs. Easton opened double doors exposing a large paneled room with moss-green walls. "Have a seat. I'll get my husband."

"Is Mariah here?" Shane asked.

Mrs. Easton nodded. "She's sleeping right now."

"Good. She could use some rest." Although Shane wanted to go to his wife, he had business to clear up first.

Cheryl Easton left, and Shane glanced around the huge room, trying to ease his nervousness. Who was he kidding? Kurt Easton had always made sure any Hunter knew his place in Haven. Hunters were blue collar. Eastons were country club. And just because Shane had married his daughter, Kurt wasn't about to give the two of them his blessing. Shane closed his eyes with a long sigh. He would do just about anything to keep Mariah. God, he couldn't lose her again.

"If you came to gloat, you can just leave." The usual authoritative voice of Kurt Easton sounded a little shaky.

Shane turned around. Although Easton had always appeared fit and much younger than his fifty-plus years, he'd seemed to age considerably in the past twenty-four hours.

"I came because the Paradise project needs to be completed on time and on budget."

Kurt glanced away. "I don't give a damn about the project. I have more pressing things on my mind."

Shane nodded. So the man was human after all. He did care about his family. "Well, I do give a damn about Paradise Estates. If it's not completed I will lose my company. So we *will* work together. And I'm not going to press charges against Rich."

Kurt's gaze darted to his. "What do you mean?"

"There's probably going to be criminal charges against your son, but he's a juvenile and will most likely get probation. All I ask from Rich is that he pay off the damages by working for me at the site."

Easton straightened. "I intend to pay the damages."

"You do, and I revoke my offer," Shane threatened. "Rich needs to be held accountable for his actions. And he needs to know that just because my name is Hunter I'm not the bad guy here."

"You're saying I am."

"I'm not playing this game, Kurt. You're the one who's kept this feud going."

"That's because it was the Eastons who lost everything."

"It was sixty years ago, for God's sake," Shane stressed. "Those people are dead and gone. As for losing everything…" He glanced around. "I'd say the Eastons have done far better than the Hunters—in material things, anyway." He stared at Easton. "So that's my offer. If you accept it, I expect to see Rich the first day of summer vacation." He headed toward the door.

"If you think this will get Mariah back, you're wrong," Easton called after him. "She won't go against me."

Shane turned around. "It's that kind of thinking that got your son into trouble. Mariah loves you, Kurt, but she also loves me. Are you're going to make her choose? If you do, in the long run she's going to hate you. You'll drive her away again."

"You're just a boy she was infatuated with in high school. She'll get over you…again."

Shane straightened. "The worst mistake I ever made was to let Mariah go. I know I hurt her, and I'll regret it forever. It was a bad time for me and my family." His dad's death had hit him hard. And his pride had been hit harder when they'd lost everything. "I love your daughter, and I'm going to do everything possible to make her happy."

"You haven't done such a great job so far."

"Then maybe you can give me a little help. My offer is on the table. It's up to you now. Are you ready to put an end to this crazy feud?

Mariah had just come down the stairs when she heard her father in his office. She walked closer and recognized Shane's voice. She began to shake. He'd come for her. Her chest tightened, making it difficult for her to take a breath. She ached to go to him, remembering when she had walked away from him and he'd called out that he loved her. How could he mean it after Rich's actions? How could he want any part of the family who tried to destroy him?

"If you love Mariah, Hunter, prove it. Walk away."

"So you're going to push family responsibility and maybe a little of your illness."

"What can I say. Mariah's a loyal daughter," her father said. "She'll never leave me while I'm ill."

Mariah had heard enough. She'd known that her father was a manipulator but this was going too far. She marched into the room. "Not as loyal as you think, Dad."

Her father looked surprised. "Mariah. You should be resting."

"I've had more than enough sleep." She turned to Shane. He looked tired, too. She doubted that he'd been to bed yet. She went to him. Not taking her gaze from her husband, she said. "Dad, I need to talk to Shane." She was shaking when she took her husband's hand. She didn't say a word until they walked through the hall to a door that went out to a brick patio.

She sucked in a breath trying to feed her starved lungs. "Did you mean what you said to me last night?"

He smiled. "All of it."

"How could you, after what—"

He stopped her words with a finger against her mouth. "You did nothing wrong, Mariah. My feelings don't depend on your family's actions."

Mariah swayed right into Shane's arms. She wrapped her arms around his neck and pulled his head down to her mouth. His lips were firm, familiar and hungry. In an instant Shane took over, deepening the kiss. Finally he broke away.

"Oh, Mariah." He scattered tiny kisses against her cheek then over her closed eyes. "I love you so much." His mouth returned to hers. She whimpered and moved against him, feeling his heat, his need for her.

"Shane. I love you, too." Her head rested against him. "I want so much to walk out of here and never look back."

"As much as I want that, too, we can't, Mariah. You need your family as much as I need mine."

Tears flooded her eyes. With the baby, they were going to have their own family, too. "What are we going to do? I want to be your wife."

He tossed her that sexy grin she loved so much. "Oh, babe, I want that, too." He leaned back, blew out a long breath. "But we can't let your father keep trying to run our lives."

She nodded. "I came out to the site last night to see you. I needed to talk to you to tell…"

His mouth captured hers again, silencing her. Lost in the kiss, she didn't want anything to spoil this. But they couldn't keep their secrets for long.

"Have you told Dad that we're married?" Mariah asked.

"Married!"

They both jerked around to see Kurt and Cheryl Easton standing in the doorway. Shane groaned. They certainly didn't need this right now, but it looked as if they didn't have any choice. He faced his father-in-law. "Yes, Mariah and I were married in Las Vegas."

Kurt glared. "The hell you were."

"Yeah, we did." He grinned. "I'm crazy about your daughter."

"And how are you going to support her?"

"Stop it, Kurt," Cheryl demanded, then turned and smiled at the couple. "Can't you see how happy they are? Everything you've done hasn't kept them apart. You lost. And if you keep being so stubborn, you're going to lose a lot more." She tossed another warning glance at her husband before she rushed to her daughter and hugged her.

"Oh, Mariah," Cheryl Easton gushed. "I wanted you to have a big wedding, but at least I can plan a reception." She had tears in her eyes as she went to Shane and hugged him, too. "I know you love her and will take care of her."

"Yes, Mrs. Easton, I do and I will."

"There's nothing more a mother could ask."

"There's a lot more," Kurt said. "Mariah, this man's construction business isn't even established."

"It is now, Dad," Mariah said. "We've been offered a job in Las Vegas."

Shane looked at his wife. "They accepted our bid?"

She nodded. "This morning. You have to call them back by tomorrow with your answer," she said, her green eyes sparkling.

"Looks like we're on our way." He kissed her tenderly. A sudden commotion broke them apart. They looked to the doorway to see the housekeeper announcing the arrival of the Hunters. Nate, Tori and Betty step through the patio door.

"We just wanted to make sure everything was okay," Betty said. "You told them about the marriage?"

Cheryl went to her guests. "Yes, it's wonderful news. We should have a toast to the newlyweds." She looked at the housekeeper. "Sarah, would you please bring in a bottle of champagne?" She glanced at Tori's rounded stomach. "Some sparkling cider, too."

"At least your mother seems happy about our marriage," Shane whispered to his bride.

She looked at her father. "It's not Mom I'm worried about."

Shane noticed that Kurt was standing alone. He still wasn't giving an inch. "I wish I could change that," Shane said."

Mariah touched his face. "I know. And I love you more for wanting to. Shane, there something else I need to tell you. Something that we didn't plan on." Her stomach clenched. "The reason I came out to see you last night is…"

The pop of a champagne cork and cheers interrupted her. The housekeeper filled the glasses and handed them out. It was Tori who brought Mariah a flute of sparkling cider. "Did you tell him?" She asked Mariah.

Shane frowned as he watched the exchange between the two women. "Tell me what?"

Mariah swallowed hard as Tori turned and left them. "Remember when we decided we should get married to stop the feud?"

"That wasn't the real reason I wanted to marry you. I loved you that night. I have forever."

"And I married you because I've always loved you. But our marriage didn't exactly end the feud."

"I know, but maybe your father will come around." Shane wasn't sure he believed that any more than Mariah did.

"How about we go a step further?" she asked.

Shane was puzzled. "Okay, but how?"

"By binding the two families together. So there's a common goal that will unite both our families once and for all."

Shane was finally getting the picture. "A baby?"

She nodded slowly. "If you remember our wedding night, we didn't exactly think about protection."

He leaned close and whispered, "Honey, you had me so crazy I wasn't—" Then it dawned on him. Mariah was pregnant. "You're already...you're having a baby?"

The conversation died as every head turned toward Mariah. She nodded. "Yes, we're having a baby. Tori came over yesterday and made me take a test to confirm what deep down I guess I already knew."

Shane pulled her into his arms and kissed her deeply. "I love you," he whispered.

"I love you, too. So you're happy about the baby?"

Shane swallowed hard, for a minute unable to describe his feelings.

"Yeah, I've never been so happy in my life," he whispered as he hugged Mariah to his side. "And this may do the trick." He raised his glass to the crowd of family. "I know it isn't customary for the groom to give the toast, but this circumstance is a little unusual. To my wife, the only woman I've ever loved." He looked down at Mariah and placed a soft kiss on her lips. Then he looked directly at Kurt Easton. "She's also just found a way to end the feud." He lifted his glass higher. "To the mother of my child. To the next generation. To our baby who is going to bring nothing but love to our families."

Shane kissed his wife again as the crowd broke out in cheers. He didn't think about Kurt, the feud or the project. As far as he was concerned, he had his own piece of paradise in his arms.

Epilogue

Six weeks later Shane watched as Nate danced Mariah around the ballroom floor at the Haven Country Club. Although he and Mariah had talked Cheryl Easton out of repeating the wedding ceremony, they relented on a reception. So here he was at the country club in a rented tux watching his beautiful wife dance with every man in the room.

But seeing how happy it made Mariah, he didn't mind one bit. She had on the same pink dress she'd worn in Las Vegas. He hadn't been able to resist her then, and he was having trouble tonight. Luckily, he didn't have to live another second without her.

The music ended and Shane made a beeline to the couple. Nate frowned at him. "I told you, I'll take good care of her. I know how to treat expectant mothers."

"You sure do," Mariah assured him.

Shane's protective instincts took over as he drew his wife to his side. "I want to be the one who takes care of you."

"And you do a great job." She turned serious. "Shane, we've talked about this before. I don't need to be coddled."

A slow ballad began, and he pulled her into his arms. "I like watching over you, Mariah. I love you."

She relaxed against him. "I love you, too. And you take care of me just fine."

"Tell that to your father. He watches me like a hawk. He's warned me that if I don't take care of you properly he'll be all over me."

Mariah's eyes sparkled. "I'm so glad that you and Dad are getting along. Well, sort of."

Shane forced a smile. "Yeah, we're workin' on it." He doubted that he would ever feel warm and cozy about the man, but they'd called a truce. Kurt had stated straight out that Shane would never be good enough for his daughter.

Shane brought his wife closer. "I'm going to prove your father wrong, Mariah."

She pulled back and smiled. "The only one you have to prove anything to is yourself. You've accomplished so much the past two years. With Paradise Estates near completion, most of the custom models already sold and the investors wanting Hunter Construction to head the next phase, I'd say you are a hot property."

Shane had been surprised when he'd been approached for another project. He'd told them that he was scheduled for the next six months in Las Vegas. "Yeah, we're both pretty hot," he said as they swayed back and forth to the music. "You're my partner, Mariah, in everything." He placed a lingering kiss on her tempting mouth.

Mariah had never been so happy in her life. She had Shane and their baby and a life together. "I like the sound of that."

"I'm just worried that, with the baby, you're trying to do too much. And we don't even have a home. My apartment is so small."

She kissed him again. "My home is anywhere you are. And we've got over six months to find another place."

"That's what I need to talk to you about," he started, then glanced up. "Uh-oh, I wonder what they want." He nodded over her shoulder. Mariah turned to see the Hunter family walking toward them. "I think it's time we made our getaway."

"Shane, that's rude. Your family just wants to share our happiness."

He groaned. "Okay, but we're out of here in ten minutes." He gave her a sexy wink. "Our honeymoon awaits."

Before Mariah could argue with Shane, his mother, Sam, Nate and Tori appeared with Emily leading the pack. His sister looked about ready to burst. "Shane, Mariah, you aren't going to believe who's starring in my movie."

"Tom Cruise?" Shane teased.

"No. Camden Peters," Emily said.

"Camden Peters!" Mariah gasped.

"Isn't it wonderful?" Tori said. "He's so sexy."

Shane looked at his brother. Nate wasn't any happier than he was that their wives were excited over some movie star.

"Hey, I heard he's nearly forty," Shane said.

His mother shot a glance at him. "Men only get better with a little age, and Camden Peters has definitely aged well."

Sam's expression said he didn't seem to like hearing about this new man coming to town. Shane had had enough, too. He took his wife's hand and pulled her away from the discussion. "Carry on," he told the group. "Mariah and I need to mingle with the other guests," he lied, as he pulled her across the dance floor.

Mariah kept up as Shane pulled her across the ballroom. Several times they were stopped and congratulated by people Shane had never met before. Finally he got his bride outside, to the deserted, moonlit balcony. This would work. He pulled Mariah into his arms and captured her mouth in a searing kiss. By the time he released her, they were both breathless and eager for more.

"Wow, that got my attention," she said. "But no, we can't leave yet. I promised Mom we'd stay until ten o'clock."

He groaned and kissed her again.

"Shane, you're not playing fair." She pushed at his chest. "You're not going to persuade me."

"I only wanted you to stop talking about that Camden guy."

"Oh, you're jealous. Just what every pregnant lady needs, especially when her waist is quickly disappearing."

His glance roamed over his tall, slender wife. "You're beautiful, even more so now that you're pregnant." He placed his hand over her flat stomach. "And no matter how round you get, you'll always be sexy to me."

Tears flooded her eyes. "Oh, Shane, I love you. I've never loved anyone except you."

He rested his forehead against hers. "Mariah...I've made so many mistakes with you. I realize now that I've always loved you, too. And I'm never going to let a day go by that I don't tell you that. And I'll do my best to be a good husband and father."

She touched his face. "You are a good husband and you will be a good father. And thanks so much for helping Rich. Because of you he's not even the same kid."

He waved off her compliment. "I'm more concerned about putting a roof over your head, providing a home for my wife and baby."

"We didn't exactly plan on a family," Mariah stated.

"Your father's wedding present might be a solution to our housing problem."

Shane wasn't sure he wanted to accept Easton's generosity, but he had a family to think about. "Your father offered us one of the model homes. Number six." He watched his wife's green eyes widen. He knew that had been her favorite design of all the models.

"Oh, Shane." She swallowed, trying to contain her excitement. "How do you feel about that?"

"At first I was upset because I'm supposed to supply a home for my family. Then I realized your father's gesture is his way of trying to make peace between the families. Now that we're tied together by this baby."

She smiled. "We are so blessed."

"I know," he said, having trouble controlling his own emotions. "Shall we accept the house on Paradise Road?"

"Sounds like a perfect place to begin our lives."

Shane drew his wife against him and captured her mouth, letting her know what she meant to him. Oh, yes, he was blessed. He had the woman he loved and a baby on the way. His business was taking off. And the Easton-Hunter feud was a thing of the past.

* * * * *

And don't miss
The next compelling episode of Patricia Thayer's
new miniseries
LOVE AT THE GOOD TIME CAFÉ
LIGHTS, ACTION...FAMILY!
(Silhouette Romance #1788)
by Patricia Thayer

Emily Hunter's only passion had been making a movie about her ancestor's frontier experiences. Then she met Reece Mckellan, a brooding Texas cowboy and his precious four-year-old niece. But for Reece, the Hunter family ranch is only a temporary stop on his way to building a family legacy of his own.

Can Emily help Reece to see that home is where the heart is and that his heart and his new family belong in Haven, Arizona, with Emily Hunter by his side?

Coming October 2005

HARLEQUIN®

N_ext™

Coming this September

In the first of Charlotte Douglas's Maggie Skerritt mysteries, an experienced police detective has to predict a serial killer's next move while charting her course for the future. But will Maggie's longtime friend and confidant add another life-altering event to the mix?

PELICAN BAY
Charlotte Douglas

If you enjoyed what you just read,
then we've got an offer you can't resist!

Take 2 bestselling love stories FREE!

Plus get a FREE surprise gift!

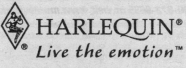

SILHOUETTE *Romance*®

COMING NEXT MONTH

#1782 THE TEXAN'S TINY DILEMMA—
Judy Christenberry
Lone Star Brides

Theresa Tyler's hidden pregnancy wouldn't prove half as difficult as interpreting the father's response. Sure, she burned for James Schofield, but she wanted to be chosen by *his* heart, not by his upright nature. Were his actions only dutiful gestures, or did something lurk beneath them? If only she could trust what *her* heart was telling her, and not her head!

#1783 PRINCE BABY—Susan Meier
Bryant Baby Bonanza

Marrying Seth Bryant only two weeks after meeting him was Princess Lucy Santos's most spontaneous moment. But when Lucy learned she was pregnant with Seth's son—her country's future king—she found herself caught up in a web of royal desires and private concerns. Would these threats blind the young couple to their original desires—or would love reign triumphant?

#1784 THE SHERIFF WINS A WIFE—Jill Limber
Blossom County Fair

When Jennifer Williams left Blossom County for the lure of big city life, Trace McCabe was crushed by the knowledge that he'd never see the love-of-his-life again. But eight years later, Jenn was back in Blossom—temporarily—to help her pregnant sister, and Trace vowed to do whatever it took to win the heart of his first love....

#1785 ONCE UPON A KING—Holly Jacobs
Perry Square: The Royal Invasion!

Three months ago Cara Phillips shared a night with a gorgeous mystery man only to find him gone when she awoke. Imagine her surprise when she shows up to serve as bridesmaid at a wedding and learns he's not only her friend's brother but a prince to boot! But will the prince ride off into the sunset once he learns Cara's most closely guarded secret—or can this fairy tale have a happy ending after all?

SRCNM0805